Selling
LipService

Selling LipService

Tammy Baikie

First published by Jacana Media (Pty) Ltd in 2017

10 Orange Street
Sunnyside
Auckland Park 2092
South Africa
+2711 628 3200
www.jacana.co.za

© Tammy Baikie, 2017

All rights reserved.

ISBN 978-1-4314-2479-5

Cover design by publicide
Set in Sabon 11/15pt
Printed and bound by Creda Communications
Job no. 002957

See a complete list of Jacana titles at www.jacana.co.za

'Chris Moulin, of Leeds University, asked 92 volunteers to write out "door" 30 times in 60 seconds. At the International Conference on Memory in Sydney last week he reported that 68 percent of volunteers showed symptoms of jamais vu, *such as beginning to doubt that "door" was a real word. Dr Moulin believes that a similar brain fatigue underlies a phenomenon observed in some schizophrenia patients: that a familiar person has been replaced by an impostor. Dr Moulin suggests they could be suffering from chronic* jamais vu.'

TIMESONLINE, 24 JULY 2006

'Man's achievements rest upon the use of symbols ... we must consider ourselves as a symbolic, semantic class of life, and those who rule the symbols, rule us.'

ALFRED KORZYBSKI

Coming of haemorrh-age

1

I have been repackaged. My cellophane surface is so slick that not even the rain clings to it. But the package contents lie. This is not what I am. The gaudy veneer of bright words that declaim and cajole are not mine – they are yours. I am the perishable rawness beneath.

You materialised with my first LipService patch. Clammy gel sucked at the skin of my upper arm, and I had to swallow hard against the rancid oil in my throat. The neurologist overseeing the hospital ward of eighteen-year-olds newly come of haemorrhage was watching me with the squinting intensity of an eye to a keyhole. He had personally applied the transdermal patch to my upper arm, while nurses went around to the other patients. Had my revulsion betrayed me? Tinnitus echoed like a siren through the empty halls of my mind. Did he know?

I remembered him as being among the group of doctors that a week or two earlier had huddled around the glow of the light boxes near the door. As they pointed and gesticulated at the brain scans, a grotesque shadow pantomime unfolded on the adjoining wall. I lay with my eyes half-closed, blinkering my mind to all but the progress of an ant across my arm and the parallel passage of bergamot that it induced across my palate. But my skin was crawling with more than six tarsal claws. I opened my eyes to see the medicine men staring at me. They had been looking into my head and seen something. Something that merited monitoring.

Now, the doctor revealed nothing. He asked how I felt, and for the first time since waking in the hospital weeks earlier, a fully formed utterance tumbled out of my throat: 'Bathed in Pristine radiance.' It was my voice but I had to turn over the strange auditory artefacts in my mind several times before admitting that they really came from me. They were not the words I had strained to reach on the high shelves of my cranium. Someone had rushed in while I groped, filled my basket with items and pushed me through the linguistic turnstile. I was left staring bewildered at the shiny word packages. That person was You.

That very first LipService patch was programmed for the Pristine bodywash brand. My response to the doctor's question was copywritten to reference the tagline: 'Remain bathed in radiance, long after you leave the tub.' Of course, I knew that greetings serve to identify a brand to interlocutors and provide a context for a speaker's LipService drift. I knew that, just as girls' bodies bleed on reaching maturity, the brain must also bleed to come of age and that after my haemorrhage I would need to consume LipService to produce language – written and spoken – like all adults. But I never really accepted that another would speak for me. Or that your tackiness would adhere to me, too.

In the months before the bloodbath in my brain, I was sure I could regain language after coming of haemorrh-age and refuse LipService as long as I retained my particular deviancy – the ability to draw up flavours through my skin. My first conscious thought on waking in a hospital bed was raw with fear that I had been flayed, in one stroke, of language and of my taste-budding skin. I roiled in the sheets, desperately trying to stir up the sediment of their aroma. At first there was nothing; my skin felt thick with tongue fur. But eventually I chilled out to the ricotta sluggishness of the bed linen. I still held the savour of myself behind pursed lips.

Was that what the doctor had been looking for, too? But instead of the perversity his eye had watered for, he had gazed on the banality of another newly bled. He had almost turned away from me when he remembered himself and said, 'Congratulations on completing neural pruning. Welcome to LipService,' patting me distractedly on the shoulder before moving off to check on the other patients.

When the doctor and nurses had gone, some of the girls in the beds on the opposite side of the room from me started chatting. The newly styled LipServants emerged from aphasia like women from beneath large bonnet hairdryers, cooing and clucking at each other in delight. Fragments of a variety of LipService brand languages floated across to me.

… wake up to the kiss of Prince coffee …
… cool mint …
… can't wait to give her the antibacterial treatment …
… so swept up in aroma'nce …
… a string of pearly whites is the best accessory…

The shy plump one on my right looked hopefully at me and was even drawing in breath to speak, but I turned on my side with my back to her. I didn't feel up to giddily pretending that You and I are the same. I wouldn't just click with You like plug and socket.

I liked them less knowing I was one of them – just as stroke-stricken, equally lost for words. We were as kinbled as our brain MRIs suggested, pinned up on the wall of the ward. Each one with an almost identical inkblot lesion – a black mark against our names and the naming of all things. I was supposed to feel bound by blood to those who shared my coming of haemorrh-age day and ward. But they were all waterslide happy to be carried along on your slippery sales pitches. And I couldn't be. Besides, with the variety of LipService patches tag-lining our tongues, we were differentiated into products: the Prince coffee girl, the Soundbites toothpaste girl, the HailChef home appliances girl … And crossing the aisle in our supermarket world is an act of treachery.

I was discharged a week later. The following months were filled with corrosive jollity – many exclamations of 'How's our new LipService mouthpiece?' Your responses were never what I had hoped for and I perpetually found myself gaping, a wound. This was just the opening that the distant aunt, family friend or neighbour was looking for to say, 'What, LipService got your tongue?' and then chortle as if this drollery weren't as tired as a face in a mirror wiped of make-up.

And these were only the preliminaries to the 'word wake' – the school graduation ceremony held once everyone in the class had bled. It's an all-night vigil for the demise of narcissistic talk and the stirring of the communal, copywritten tongue. As instructed in the invitations, my classmates and I arrived without wearing the transdermal patches we'd needed since our haemorrhages. We stood in the school hall, a row of mutes dressed in white – the blank pages of a sheaf. The teachers filed past, shaking each individual's hand and penning a LipService wish on our clothing. Next came the parents, who did the same.

'Receive the script,' said the principal, placing a wafer with the word 'copywritten' on our tongues. The wafer melted away but the letters left a stain that lasted more than a week. For all its superficiality, the brand chatter programmed into the LipService patch indelibly marks both body and mind.

There was a cheer from the audience as the hall was plunged momentarily into darkness, before the glow of black lights came on at exactly the same moment as the sound of a loud jingle. Our white clothes phosphoresced blue-opal. Then our line dissolved as friends and family advanced and neat ceremonial script gave way to frenzied scrawlings. Marker pens snagged and puckered skin, disembodied hands of the dancing crowd reached, wrote and withdrew. I had no LipService patch, no words to protest. Arms raised defensively presented another surface for phrases that ran into each other, knocking themselves insensate, and in the rush to find a footing on the body, meaning slipped and was trampled. Letters piled up, a writ of passage into branded language.

At midnight, the lights were switched back on and the music stopped. Dazzled by the brightness, I glanced down at my dress – white no more. We were pushed forward again. 'You have received the script. Now speak your part,' intoned the principal as she approached the line of new LipServants that had reformed. She ceremonially handed each of us a LipService patch.

Disoriented, we were herded off to the photographer to have our pictures taken with a stuffed parrot perched on a shoulder. One of its glass eyes was chipped and this gave it a duplicitous expression. It was supposed to represent Polly, the LipService mascot, which appears on the cover of LipService catalogues in the form of a tattooed bird and logo on a naked shoulder. Whenever I look at the photo of me taken that night, it strikes me that the scribbling covering my clothes and body is a double exposure – a second competing image. The startled girl beneath is dematerialising, to leave only the tatty parrot and its lines.

At dawn I lay in the bath, the hot water needling hide scrubbed raw but still not entirely clean. Traces of marker pen appeared like meat stamps on the tenderised loin.

These memories are as abrasive as my fingernail scraping over the backing of the LipService patch – that cheerfully printed polyester scab on my shoulder. By goading that circle of skin back to sensation, perhaps I could reawaken the dead spot in my brain. It's the moribund places that You insinuate yourself into.

I wish I could tell You how much I loathe You. For a long time, I contemplated curses so pustular You would break out in boils at the sound of them. Only they'll never be heard. All LipService products block obscenity. And to whom would I address my rage anyway? I'm left looking on helplessly at the endless treachery of the impostor wearing my skin.

Then it came to me that I could interrogate You. You wouldn't answer directly but I already know all your answers, because You are perfect conformity. Beneath the dome of my skull, where my inner voice is now forever trapped, my word is still law. Here, I can put You in the dock.

I try to picture You bowed and crumpled but I can't see your features. No amount of swivelling of the mind's inner periscope brings You into focus. You remain a blur of peripheral vision. 'Show me your face,' I hiss. The words have barely rumbled loose and already I know the answer – you are a boardwalk billboard painted with strong men flexing their muscles. Where the bodybuilders' heads are, there are holes for people like me to stick our faces through. Your face is mine. But I don't want to be a caricature, nor do I want to be stuck in the shadows behind the board, where lost shoes lie after falling from the feet of children craning to hook their chins into the cutout.

'Don't like what you see, my pet?'

You're speaking Love Bites pet food. Since that's my current patch, it's natural for You to speak that brand, even in my head, but 'my pet'? It's the Love Bites expression that makes me feel like I've bitten into an ice cube every time it comes out of my mouth. I'm supposed to be in control of your words. Where did that come from?

'Stop trying to convince me that You and I are one and the same. I know what You are. You are nothing but the programmed response to a combination of drugs and electrical stimulus activated by nanotechnology.'

'Just an involuntary twitch of a tail, eh? Aren't I so much more?'

'Fine. You're the leash that the corporates have tightened around my throat.'

'Oh mee-ow. LipService speech is created by copywriters to declaw breeds like you.'

'I refuse to be one of those creatures that sit and beg for your scraps.'

'You have clearly failed to appreciate the catechism. LipService is not scraps, it provides a wholesome mental balance and contains all the positive sentiments scientifically proven to keep you living a healthier, fuller life. The well-socialised animal is happier and less prone to illness.'

'I'm not one of your carbon copycats, I'm not ...'

'And yet you're speaking Love Bites LipService. In your own head. Did you forget which of us was which?'

That's not how this was supposed to go. Panic feels like being vacuum packed. But You continue talking:

'Or did it just seem natural, like the nutritious ingredients in Love Bites? One bite and you're smitten, eh? Common expression is social grooming. But you're not a pally cat. Oh no, you think you've got it all licked – a special feeline. But this cat's got your tongue.'

I'm hyperventilating. I scramble for a shopping bag and breathe into it. That wasn't just me imagining You. No, You are the copywriter's familiar who stalks my every thought.

I rip off the Love Bites patch and stamp on it. It oozes bile from the drug reservoir like a crushed earwig.

Before the haemorrhage

2

Her long fingernails were painted with miniature logos, perfect in every detail. Their length meant that Mrs Mondaine handled everything, including our marked tests, with a funny tweezing action. It reminded me of Mother plucking her eyebrows – from the frowny grip, through ouchy rip, to the let slip. The pincers released my results onto my desk and I saw four brand hero stickers attached to the top. Four! I felt breakfast-cereal-cartoon perky.

I was ten and I was probably wearing my favourite T-shirt, which said 'Little Madams' just above the small brass cones at nipple height with tassels sprouting from them. I was always wearing that. Hanging upside down from the playground jungle gym, I would swish-swish them like *la femme* Frisson Froufrou from the ad, who dangled from a trapeze and whose bustier tassels flicked as she swung. I was going to be spotlit beautiful like her and like Mother, who is a sales manager for the lingerie brand. By learning the right figure-hugging LipService, I was going to follow her into the embrace of the Frisson Froufrou brand family. Or maybe even be a copywriter. Then I would write the grown-ups' clever LipService words that wiggle up into your bum like my Butt'fly G-string (a gift from Mother) and stick there so you can't forget them. But Mother said we weren't an ebrandgelical family. Then she looked hard at Dad. Still, with four brand hero stickers, I thought they'd let me.

The brand awareness lesson that day was on quality. Mrs Mondaine passed fabric samples around the class: 'If it feels as good as silk, cashmere or linen to the touch and looks as good, well then it must be as good.' I raised my hand. I imagined myself as Stainley, the Cryowash stain detective, who uncovered the dirt that everyone else had overlooked.

'Mrs Mondaine, you can taste the difference between the real silk and Selkie.'

Mrs Mondaine had the face of an inflatable doll. Her eyes narrowed so that the heavy mascara on her lashes formed puckers around the dark orifices in her head. I thought there must be some LipService drift I had forgotten, and continued: 'I mean, the taste you get when you touch something, which makes it easier to tell what it is – you know, metal is like salad dressing – and Selkie is ...'

'I don't understand your value-added contribution, Frith,' she said.

The other kids were staring at me. My confidence curled at the edges, brand hero stickers that no longer adhered properly. It felt like looking down into the emptiness of Mother's bra cups when I first snuck into her cupboard to try on her things. I thought that everybody could taste things through their skin, that they all picked at the walnuts in lace. Wasn't that as ordinary as haemorrhages, health rewards and brand awareness lessons?

'The core sensory competency of the skin is not taste, Frith. Did you put the samples in your mouth?'

'No, Mrs Mondaine. I felt them and tasted them through my skin.'

'That is false advertising. Make a full retraction.'

'But Mrs Mondaine ...'

Mrs Mondaine took me to the principal's office. She said nothing as we walked, but the sound of her heels on the corridor made the same noise as coins fed into slot machines. Every step made my head spin symbols – lace, walnut, Frisson Froufrou – but they were all unlucky combinations.

I had never been to see Principal Launder before. Mrs Mondaine left me in a small room with a table and two chairs. It was the barest room I had ever been in. No windows, no posters or pictures, no mobiles or collections of brand figurines. That made me more frightened than I already was. There was nothing to distract me from the horrible scrabble to understand. I picked at a scab on my knee until it bled. I stroked at the corduroy of my pinafore but its furry guava only reminded me of what I'd said before Mrs Mondaine pulled me from my desk. I twisted at a button on my cardigan until the thread broke and I had to put it in my pocket.

Then I heard it – Mrs Mondaine's casino clack. There was another sound, too, a soft flip of notes shuffled – the big money. I froze. But the door didn't open. There were voices out in the corridor, Mrs Mondaine and Principal Launder. I got up from the chair and stood still, barely breathing. Slowly, I edged towards the door and pressed myself to the wood whose sour rye trickled into my ear and down my throat.

I yanked my mind loose from the taste and texture of the door and concentrated on the voice, which whined like the TV test pattern.

'What if there is a fault with the metrics on the cohort's perception of the quality experience? It could damage the credibility of the brand promise with a knock-on-effect for reputation management.'

'Mrs Mondaine,' Principal Launder said, 'you are mistaking an anomaly for actionable market intelligence.'

'Even if we don't send a risk report to the corporation, we must surely submit her for biomedical recall?'

'An unnecessary escalation. We can correct any behavioural flaws through peer reconditioning. You will discuss this incident with the rest of the cohort using the psychological cues I've copywritten for you, and social pressure will correct the cognitive dissonance.'

Then there was the sound of feet moving, and I threw myself across the room to reach the chair and table. If the principal saw my dive for the desk, he didn't show it. Leaning forward, he put on a pair of spectacles and said, 'Ah, you must be Frith's friend, Faith.' When he spoke his voice was smoothy perfect like it had been airbrushed. I didn't know anyone called Faith but nodded, unsure whether it was a game or whether he honestly thought I was someone else. Either way, it felt safer than being me.

'So you would know about her tasting things she touches?' Another nod. Being Faith made things much easier. Next, he asked whether Frith could hear colours. I must have looked surprised, so he changed the question to whether sounds had colours. And what about tastes, did they have textures? No. Well then, I had to agree that tasting through skin, as Frith said she did, seemed made up. All her other senses functioned alone. I understood now. To admit to being Frith or that Frith really could taste things she touched made me a liar. What could I say when he asked if I would help to convince Frith to stop pretending? Didn't I see that her game of make-believe was not very credible, and it was dangerous – she must be made to realise that it was false advertising and defamation of Selkie. My 'yes' was more like the little sssss when opening almost-flat cola. He wanted to know whether I thought she would continue with such slander. The bones in my neck made gristle grindings against the shaking of my head.

I didn't like being Frith any more. I wished I were Faith. Principal Launder trusted her to be a good consumer.

I was allowed to go. It was lunchtime. Outside the windowless room, colour had drained from the world. Bleached litter trapped in tree branches on the playing fields flapped like prayer rags.

I kept picking apart my talk with the principal, trying to understand his magic tricks – how with his talk of Frith and Faith, he had performed the famous sawing-a-girl-in-half illusion. I realised that he meant for me to overhear his discussion with Mrs Mondaine. The top-hat words that things disappeared into were all part of the abracadabra. He was probably a burned-out copywriter – most headmasters are. And, of course, what I didn't understand at the time was that my two halves would never fit back together.

In the canteen, there were hardly any kids still in the queue to collect the sponsored lunch hampers. I was walking away from the refrigerated shelves when one of the girls from my class came up to me and dropped a used handkerchief into my Big Chief Beef Bolognese. 'Wouldn't you rather eat this?' she said, before walking away. There was the sound of sniggers.

The handkerchief joke was repeated and then I started receiving little fabric dolls with anatomical details crudely drawn in marker pen and a plastic speech bubble stuck to the mouth saying things like 'lick me'. Some time later, one of the teachers found me choking on a dirty sock that a group of older kids had shoved into my mouth.

My visit to the principal was never mentioned at home, although my mother as the brand-affiliated parent must have been notified. She was as consoling as my talking Gabby doll. Tug at the cord in her back and Mother would say the sweetest things to distract me from the questions she couldn't or wouldn't answer. 'Need a little lift, darling? Shoulders back, chest out – it's an instant push-up.' But I knew that the incident frayed at the fibres of my mother's hopes for me, because although she still spoke the words, tugging her LipService cord now elicited warbling that lacked conviction. The ballad of *la femme* Frisson Froufrou played like a stretched tape now that she had failed to socialise me in the ways and words of the brand.

Mother is a believer. Her brand loyalty is a neon example at BMG Textile and Clothing Corporation. Nothing but Frisson Froufrou crosses her heart, crotch or lips – even when off work she only uses FF patches.

She spent years cultivating her image, only to find I had sprouted in ways incompatible with the BMG corporate and social culture. I had issued from her like a black bush of armpit hair above her beribboned corsetry. She'd always have to keep her arms stiffly clamped to her sides, hiding that shaggy shame.

Everybody knows it's the parents' role to pass on by word of mouth the values and LipService of their corporate tribe. Then when the child comes of haemorrh-age and the blood knot is broken, the transition to the family brand and patched speech comes as naturally as swiping a credit card.

She wouldn't willingly have taken me out of the BMG-sponsored school but she was informed that my 'poor fit with the corporate identity' was undermining brand integrity in the classroom, and the administration could not accept responsibility for my safety. Dad wasn't employed by a corporation and, without a second brand affiliation in the family, the only alternative was the 'no-name' school. I sighed into anonymity. No focused brand identification courses, no corporate mascots at sports events and little prospect of internships or admission to the corporate universities. I would certainly never be a copywriter.

3

The dressing-up box was an old trunk full of cast-off chiffon slips, satin cami sets and babydolls Mother had put together so that I could learn to be a Frisson Froufrou lady. When I needed close and tender comfort, I would take everything off, climb in and close the lid to enjoy the whiskery ribbons and slippery fabrics tonguing alfalfa and sesame on my belly and back. But then Faith told on me to Principal Launder. When I had to leave the BMG-sponsored school, Mother stopped inviting me to play Demoiselles de FF. She probably thought it had become a pointless exercise.

I told myself I didn't mind, because I was trying to forget the dressing-up box and ignore skin tastes. They were pretend – a game I forgot to stop playing. Like when I used to believe that *the* Peppy the Crayon Clown came to my fourth birthday party, instead of someone paid to put on a costume. But when did I first make them up? What was the first stroking that I invented a taste for? I couldn't find that lost moment or imagine how I'd lost it.

Skin tastes had simply always been there, like arms and legs. When I was seven, our class went to the Animal Crackers petting zoo and I touched a snake for the first time. Between contact and liquorice there was no time. No time to think of favourite foods or fancy flavours. Even now, with my mind running, running red rover towards the fault – which had to be there – between finger and flavour, all I managed was to knock myself to pieces. I was fracturing trying to get through the impasse. Nothing made sense, and I was afraid that I wouldn't be able to switch the skin tastes off. And that I wouldn't be able to go back to being the product of an endorsed family.

Inside my brain was a wall of TVs, each with a different grown-up – Mother, Mrs Mondaine, Peppy the Crayon Clown – competing to tell me how their brand could fix me. I put my head under my bed, willing myself to pinch my pores closed against the stinky blue-cheese synthetic carpet, and howled, 'Not real, not real. I don't taste anything!' The scream was an electrical surge that blanked the screens. Only one small voice was left.

'Oh, hardly anything is real any more. Everyone is pretending all the time – being a play-play *la femme* Frisson Froufrou or whatever. But you can't just invent your own fantasy world. There are rules, silly-that's-what-you-get-when-you-eat Chilli Fusilli.' It sounded like me, only copywriter clever. That's how I knew it was Faith.

Of course, Faith was make-believe, but I wanted to believe. I wanted to be sure of things, the way she was. Everyone needs a brand conscience – that's why there are relationship management days at schools, when you introduce your imaginary brand buddy. At my new school, it was just two months away, not long after my eleventh birthday. Everyone would see how, with Faith, my pretend was really intend. I might even be able to make the early adopters programme. That's how Mother started at Frisson Froufrou.

'So what games are allowed?' I asked.

Faith rolled her eyes. 'You know, playing proper brand characters.'

It was Faith's idea to try the black satin Lycra opera gloves that came with an old peignoir in the dressing-up box. The fingers were a little too long and they hung off my hands like skin gone wrinkly from swimming. But they did gag the skin tastes. When I first put the gloves on, the singed sesame force-fed itself down my throat. After a while I became numb to it, the way when sitting in a room with a wet dog, the nose quickly forgets how a room without a wet dog smells.

'You must wear them all the time,' Faith said.

'What about eating? And bathing?'

'For eating, too. S'pose you'll have to take them off for washing though.'

'But bathwater is lovely pink Turkish delight ...'

'You're not trying hard enough, Frith. If you can't block out the Turkish delight in the bath, then it should at least be Pasha's Pleasure and you should hum the turban tune. Engage with Pasha's brand story and commodeify, commodeify.'

That was Faith – constantly telling me what to do: 'You have to live brand culture, not just act all diligent in class,' and 'Come on, wear their art on your sleeve, merchandise your look.' She was always right and I was always wrong. And we always had to do what Faith wanted. She refused to come with me to the book repository. 'Aggh, it's so depressing – no flash and attention grab.'

But at least she was there with me the first day I wore the gloves to school. Even though it was summer, I wore tights with a dress and the long black satin cuffs that reached up to my armpits to smother the seductions of skin. I knew what everyone was thinking: What *is* the new girl wearing? That's not catalogue cool – bet that's not in any season's collection. She's got no idea about strategic alignment. What a surprise she ended up in a no-name school.

The glove days wore on and wore down. I was a cat with clipped whiskers, never sure of the places I could fit, bumping into things. In the evenings, I peeled off the gags and my skin screamed mouthfuls. Standing naked in the steam coming off the water in the tub, I was a satellite dish of flavours amplified. I took long gluttonous baths, soaking up sweet rose water. The gloves worked while they were on but when they came off, I seemed to be worse – with a thirsty proboscis protruding from every follicle. Faith said it was the lie of skin tastes coming out, like when junkies go cold turkey.

I wanted to show Faith that I also had core competencies – that I could talk LipService lickety-split and was copywriter clever. And, while I was having one of my very long baths, I found a way to do it. I was trying to think of Pasha's Pleasure like Faith said I should, but my mind kept diving after playful Pobbles because Dad had given me funny poems to read in the book repository. So every now and then I had to chant to myself Pasha's Pleasure, Pasha's Pleasure, Pasha's Pleasure until it got all gargoyled up into Shapa's Sureplea. I thought that was quite funny, too. That's what I'd call a Turkish delight that you can only eat in the bath. The silliness went ricocheting through my head and upset the neat order until it lodged in an idea. What if I made up a LipService with special secret words? Everyone knows that shared LipService is a cohesive force that engenders mutual consciousness among brand communities of haemorrh-aged. It's catechism.

All I needed was a brand, something to sell. What did I have to sell? I couldn't think of anything. I almost asked Faith but I wanted to have it all worked out myself before I told her.

It was obvious, really. If I was going to create a sort of secret language, why not sell the words to my classmates? That's not so different to LipService, is it? It's a tried-and-tested business model. I was so proud of myself. There would be words for ordinary things like teachers (shirties) or parents (rent pairs) so they wouldn't know when we were talking about them, and words for things that just deserved to have a single expression, like 'on an urchin quest' (from questioner), referring to someone like my dad who never sounded convinced by their own LipService. I could call my language Wardsback because the words were roughly reversed versions of familiar ones, and they pushed back at the old meanings the way wearing a woolly jumper back to front tugs at the throat and armpits.

Faith played with her hair for a long time when I told her about the idea, and I felt like a piece of CheezPleez left in the sun – dry and curling at the edges and sweaty in the middle. She probably didn't believe that any of my ideas could be buyonormative. But she couldn't think of any reason to junk it and she got more and more excited about making money with absolutely no overheads.

I remember the first word I sold was 'ox parade' (from paradox) for when a grown-up's LipService drift seemed to say one thing but you were pretty sure they meant another. Poppy, who smelled of condensed milk, bought it, which was surprising because she was really quiet. I wrote the words and their definitions on old LipService patch backings, folded them up and put them in a jar. The customer stuck a hand in and pulled one out. Faith insisted that we charge a minimal one-off subscription per user over and above the original buyer.

'Who cares about that?' I said. 'Wouldn't it be lexicool if the other kids used my words? And besides, how would we ever keep track of who was allowed to use which words?'

'That's the genius of the haemorrhage and LipService, isn't it? Built-in control. I'll just have to work on an accounting system.'

I didn't know how her head, which was mine, could ever possibly hold all those columns and double entries. But I needed her approval.

I hadn't been sure if Poppy liked her word, until I overheard her best friend whisper to her in a corridor, 'Ms Marshal put on a real ox parade in there over contrabrand. What was she trying to say?'

'Oh, who knows? The bull really had her by its horns,' Poppy replied and they both tittered.

They were using my word! I had my gloves on but I was doused in the shiver and prickle of ginger ale, my skin goosed in mimicry of the bubbles. There were more buyers every day after that – in fact I had a hard time thinking up enough words for all the kids that crowded around my table at lunch wanting to dip into the 'gun jar' (jargon). Some of the words were duds but I thought quite a few were really great, like 'lexity perp' (from perplexity) for an adult whose LipService was complete gibberish, 'showman pros' (from promotions) for kids who were already so into their chosen brand they made the rest of us look like flip-floppers and 'get tarred' (from targeted) referring to the kids who just couldn't wrap their heads around brand awareness.

I even stopped missing the skin tastes. I could go almost a whole day without thinking about them until it came to the Turkish delight hour. With Wardsback, each of my words echoed off all those other tongues. I was no longer a singularity; I was we, the multiplicity. I felt large, bigger than the other kids. And I was doing big things. There was quality control – not just of the words themselves but also listening out to make sure no one was using them incorrectly or unrightfully. To help with that we had 'fire nutties' (notifiers) who rather enjoyed watching others get burned. They were paid to eavesdrop on schoolyard conversations. Based on their intelligence, the 'wrist rotors' (terrorists) could be sent in to twist arms and punish offenders.

I know I should've thought more about all that. Somehow it just grew out of Faith's subscription programme, the way in winter you forget to cut your toenails until one spring day you find you have hideous claws that rake anyone who stands too close. I tell myself I didn't actively set it all up. I don't remember recruiting. But I came up with the names. Is naming something the same as assuming responsibility for it?

I was not myself any more. My image had come unstuck – a promotional cardboard cutout was walking around instead of me. In the corridors, I would pass younger girls wearing tights with dresses and long opera gloves. They did their hair like me, plaiting the forelock and tucking it behind an ear. At lunch, they only ate what I ate. Once, I noticed one of them mimicking the way I carried my schoolbag and my nervous habit of nibbling the uninhabited fingertip of my glove. It was a hall of mirrors – everywhere I saw myself, disembodied. Even Faith had stopped lecturing me. 'These are the rewards of a strong brand,' she said between cooing sweet numbers over the day's takings.

Did I enjoy it? I keep asking myself. I want to say no, but that's probably a lie. I was the Wardsback girl and everyone knew the Wardsback girl. I was greater than the sum of my many refractions. When the others came to buy words, there was the way they looked at me. And the way they spoke my words. A clandestine tone like the hiss of a graffiti can. I didn't see that I was in a market bubble.

The wrist rotors got carried away with a kid called Ansgar and dislocated his finger. Somehow in my memory he seems connected to Poppy – like a cousin or a brother's friend. But I think that's just the vanity of guilt, the need for what came next to be a personal punishment and not just inevitable market forces. Poppy started selling words. Hers were cheaper. There was no secondary-user subscription and no enforcers, although she would've probably gotten there, too. What was hardest for me was that her words were good – like 'frenvy' for when a friend gets an iconic product that you desperately want, and the fact that they have it and you don't makes it hard for you to continue liking them.

Not all of the Wardsback customers disappeared straight away.

But another one or two kids started peddling words not long after Poppy. Soon profits crashed and my social stock fell. The opera gloves and tights of the Wardsback ebrandgelists vanished from the school hallways. I looked around for direction but, as the Wardsback star faded, I lost my bearings. I had rewired my night sky as advertising hoardings.

Faith said we would cut the competition down with our wrist rotors. I would need to start working on a series of tarnish words referring to speakers of other brands. They would see that only the business with a viable retention strategy survives. Ours was the superior brand. Only I didn't feel very superior. My words didn't seem better than Poppy's. I was groping. Brands were slippery things – Selkie could become silk and my game of words a corporate crackdown. I missed the palpable pawing reality of my skin tastes, where things pressed up close and declared from my throat what they were. The order for the sear and smear campaign never went out.

There were so many new words and so many kids using them that the teachers realised what was going on. An assembly was called and the headmistress announced, 'Almost all of you without exception have been involved in the trafficking and proliferation of contrabranded language, which undermines the efforts of this institution to prepare you for life post-haemorrhage and brand-self integration, in particular. The faculty is forced to implement corrective measures. A two-week gag order will be implemented, with immediate effect. After that, a new batch of personality and brand matchmaking tests will be conducted.'

As we filed out of the hall, a doctor and nurse were waiting at the door to administer vocal-inhibiting injections.

This was exactly the kind of thing Faith was supposed to warn me about before I started Wardsback. She was supposed to keep me out of trouble. Instead I had caused all this. Teachers often threatened us with gag orders but I'd never heard of it actually happening – and to the whole school. How had we gotten it so wrong?

Faith was sullen. 'We didn't. We did everything exactly the way they do it. That's what they didn't like. If you'd done what I told you and sent out the wrist rotors, we could've regulated the market and controlled use. You just couldn't handle the business behind branding.'

In fact, I wasn't sure I liked Faith any more. I told her to leave me alone. We were no longer friends, and I wasn't introducing her as my imaginary brand buddy at school. I never spoke to Faith again. But I was wrong to think that Faith would just go away. Faith has come back, only now instead of me speaking for her, she speaks for me. You are Faith.

Ripping off opera gloves, kicking off tights, flinging off my dress, I climbed into the dressing-up box and cried for a long time. I cried for a whole school of kids who walked through hallways making only sad herd sounds – snufflings, scratchings, huffings. And I cried for myself because no matter how hard I tried to be good, I seemed to be bad. Now I had no voice and no choice. But the words were still there, small pale insects scuttling about. And just like Poppy and her clever words, it just popped into my head.

'Tasture.' That's what skin tastes should be called. I had stopped crying, and the new word rustled around the alfalfa of Mother's rich satin nightie and stirred again when sesame chiffon brushed my face. It wasn't a word I planned on ever telling anyone, and, besides, no one would be making words any more. So what did it matter that I'd used Poppy's word-making technique?

I got out of the dressing-up box and found a pair of scissors. There might not be any paper any more, except in the repository, but I was going to make a book – a secret book. I cut Mother's old lingerie into rectangles and stitched the pieces together along one side. I would write stories on the pages, about the pages.

4

I spent afternoons at the end of the school day at the book repository waiting for Dad to finish work. Almost no one went there except the vacuum-sealed vans carrying volumes that had been hidden in walls and floors, buried in containers of rice, sewn into furniture upholstery or taped to the owner's body. It had been decades since the doctors discovered the deadly library mould and ordered the sequestration of all printed literature, but still the vans kept arriving with confiscated tomes. I couldn't understand why people still sicked to death because of those things, when everyone knows books bring the wheezing, blue-veined end of breath. I only ever visited the exhibits in the reception area, staring at the stifled volumes set in blocks of resin and sealed in display cases together with magnified slides of microbes and photos of patients in the respiratory wards. I stared through glass and time at the dusty galaxies of green-black spores on the open pages, trying to read the words so different from any brand of LipService. Every day I stared and felt the air sucked out of the present.

Dad found me one afternoon, trying not to breathe and fog the glass. 'Ah, it's an airtight case,' he said with that wry expression he had when he used LipService in ways that felt like putting a shoe on the wrong foot. 'We glazed over books, then eyes glazed over. Would you to like to see more?'

'More books? Won't they make me sick?'

'No, no, we'll put you in a nice dust jacket.'

Then, for the first time, he took me in the lift down to the hermetic underground vaults. He showed me how to put on the hooded plastic suit and mask, which rustled up runny egg yolks in my mouth, and we stepped into the airlock. On the other side of the door was a former underground grain silo. I stood peering under the crinoline that covered society's nether regions. Books lined the walls of the floodlit well, which was hooped with tiers of balconies rising eighty metres up. Freestanding shelves conferred in the centre of the shaft, casting deep shadows as they leaned into each other on their ladders. At the opposite end of the silo from the airlock door, a tunnel led to a succession of four more identical silos. Imagining the billions of letters spun into words, spun into sentences, felt like an enormous centrifugal force: I didn't think I'd be able to make my way to the middle of such a vast swirl of minutiae.

'How many are there?' I whispered, staring up.

'Books? About eleven and a half million.'

'Why do we keep them if they're poisonous?'

'Copywriters used to come. Not so much any more.'

'But all the books are digitised, we don't need these.'

'You keep referencing the case in reception.'

My thoughts teetered on the edge of a bluff. He continued, 'Come, let me explain the science of authority control.'

On the second-tier balcony, Dad pulled out a slim picture book entitled *The Emperor's New Clothes* by Hans Christian Andersen. 'Read this, I'll be back in a while.' His footsteps on the steel stairs up to the higher decks sounded like the metallic shutout of gates barring storefronts at night. I didn't want to be left alone. I was afraid of the books. The colours slapped me down; there was no commercial clowning. I was sure this was the place of no escape – not even for microbes. I opened the book with clumsy gloved fingers. The pages sprayed like the hair of a trampolinist.

The paper was different from the glossily coated and laminated kinds that you sometimes still find in packaging. It looked breathing, like skin. There was no smudge of mould on any of the pages. I wanted to touch one, to know it at the base of my tongue, but I thought of the exhibit above me and its photos of the sick, who I was sure had green cobwebs in their lungs.

I found myself starey, facing the pictures of the emperor and the weavers. I couldn't understand why they looked wrong. It wasn't the funny clothes or that the pictures were neither cartoons nor photos. There was something about it, like the too-tight smile some grown-ups cracked at kids.

When Dad returned, he asked if I recognised the story. I said no, because I hadn't ever heard of the Hans Christian Andersen corporation or its brands. He had that sad face I remembered from when Mother trade-dressed the tree in our yard in Frisson Froufrou.

'Hans Christian Andersen is the copywriter, Frith. So what is the brand?'

I didn't know. 'Weavers,' I said and felt stupid.

'Are you sure there is one?'

No brand. It was even more unimaginable than the upside-down, back-to-front world of the Freaker Sneakers advergame that lets your avatar walk on the ceiling. I didn't believe anything was possible without brands – even the wildest fantasy.

After a long pause, Dad said, 'What if this book were indexed together with *CEO Sindy's Selkie Suit?*'

Almost every second night, Mother used to read to me about how Selkie was invented. The paper book was the same story as the BMG textile corporation's brand narrative, except for the ending. Instead of the textile technologists teaching CEO Sindy and the management board about fabric quality so that Selkie is no longer invisible to them, the emperor is laughed at as he parades naked through the street. That wasn't branding the bright side. The harder I tried to understand the differences, the more I was reminded of the day with Mrs Mondaine and the headmaster.

Squirming in the biohazard suit made it twist and tighten around me. Sweat made the plastic cling, and egg yolks oozed slimily down my throat. I towed my attention back to my father, trying to listen, trying to hear sense.

'In authority control, multiple writers, here Andersen and his sources, are reduced with controlled vocabulary into a single catalogue access point, the authorised file '*CEO Sindy's Selkie Suit*, BMG corp. copyright', which is the only version licensed for electronic publication.'

Some of the LipService words he was using were difficult to understand. So I tried to explain it to myself out loud.

'Other people never get to read the stories as they are down here.'

'No.'

I remembered a word from brand awareness: proprietorship. I don't know if I understood even then that what the narrative lacked was a corporate context. For me, the story whirled away like water down the drain because there was no branded identity plugging its centre. How could I grasp it if I didn't know which entity held it as property, had owned and trademarked it? While the underground silo and the book didn't fit with our consumerism, I recognised exclusivity when I saw it. Mother had made sure of that. Only the very few can have the magical things that transform you.

Above all, the language was a wild rushing in my ears.

'Can I come back?' I asked Dad.

'Only if you make no citations or cross-references to the silos or books.'

I could see he was smiling behind the mask.

For the next six years, I went underground, spending almost every afternoon down in the silos. Sometimes, I would see Dad already in there. Sometimes, he left a book for me on the floor near the door. None of the books showed the green-black taint like the one in the display case. I became sloppy about the biohazard suit until I stopped wearing it completely.

I inhaled mouldy words that grew into the breathy mycelium of story colonies. In the subterranean silos, they spread over my childhood brand narratives and decomposed them; at the slightest stirring, the downy must of language released puffs of sporious unbranded tellings.

5

The cover had the grain, colour and gloss of spilled flaxseed. It still answered with the animal heat of being hidden under my shirt. My fingers moved intently over the Brailleish bumps of its surface, imbibing its report of squid ink. No other old leather binding had ever painted my tongue paella black before. As I lifted the cover, which read, in gold lettering, *Elementary Treatise on Human Anatomy*, it made the electric crackle of a loose connection. Inside, a bookplate marked 'Ex Libris Dr Ungar Sever' showed a brain under a bell jar. Anyone would recognise the name of the neuroscientist instrumental in the development of the LipService patch. But he couldn't have been the first to own the book, as the date at the top of the frontispiece was 1869. Below was an inscription:

> This book is bound in the hide of an indigent, one Eda-Lyn, who died at the almshouse. On conducting the autopsy, I discovered *Taenia solium* – the same bladder worm recently proven by Dr Friedrich Küchenmeister to be the juvenile form of the pork tapeworm – encysted in the tissue. Having seen the patient devouring ham and bologna sausage brought by a visiting relative in a singularly undainty fashion, I theorised a connection between her intemperate consumption and her death, and presented my findings as my first humble contribution to the *Journal of Medicine*. Thus, at least in death the parasitic classes contribute to the improved health of society. I flayed and dressed the skin according to the tanner's art before handing it to a bookbinder.
>
> Dr Emmet Skinner

I wanted to drop it but I couldn't just let the last book that my dad gave me – and the only book I've ever taken from the repository – fall. My fingernails clenched around it, like teeth holding it away from the tongue, until I could finally release it safely. Trying to wipe away the black staining taste, my hands grazed heavily at my thighs, soothing and satisfying myself on the warm chanterelle mounds of my skin. Across from me was Eda-Lyn – perfectly cured. Why was this afflicted textual body the last thing that Dad put into my hands?

Five months were left before my eighteenth birthday and the rupture was coming some day soon. Even if it's just a tiny rip in an artery wall, it might as well be one of those portholes – fistulas – they cut in the side of cows so they can keep shoving things in and pulling them out. Swivelling eyeball to the glass, the wearers of rubber gloves make sure the herd has a belly full of trademarked enzymes, which can digest the corporate message good and proper. The only difference is we cover our holes with patches.

Lying on my back in bed at night, I groped for that bulging aneurysm in a cerebral artery. I wanted to probe it and have it answer back with sensation like wiggling a loose tooth. But I couldn't grasp it. All I ended up with was an impossible-to-pinpoint headache. The rupture is the unspeakable divide – no one's words live to tell the tale. Ask anyone who has come of haemorrh-age what the bleed is like, and the answer is always exactly the same: *For our share of mind we receive brand equity – our place in and piece of the capital. We have our premises; finally, we belong. We can never again be misunderstood. So there is fulfilment in our every fleeting fad.* It's catechism – the social principles programmed into every patch irrespective of branding. Only it doesn't answer the question. It says nothing about how it feels for the power grid to fail in a whole district of the brain, reducing it to candles and a Primus stove.

I asked Dad about it. He started to rattle off the catechism, then stopped suddenly. Taking one of the copies of *Great Expectations*, he ripped out pages and randomly stuffed them back between the others before handing me the book. Holding the disordered sheets, a sickbed of incoherent narrative, I felt a cold intravenous drip of fear.

My classmates were all really hyped about haemorrh-aging. Osric was the first to bleed. It happened during a lesson on a day I skipped school to read at the book repository. I would've done that more often if I hadn't been afraid the teachers would notice and start investigating, but I was sorry to have missed Osric's rupture. The other kids didn't seem to have been paying attention to the stuff I was interested in. Most of their talk was about how he'd managed to be the first. Some said it was the weird neck stretches everyone saw him doing several times a day – right arm over the top of his head so the hand covered his left ear and his head tilted to the right. Then he'd switch to the opposite side. Others said it was because he had built an affiliation to a non-consumer tech brand – something to do with plant automation – and the company had decided to fast-track him. None of it made much sense, but everyone was incentivised and neck stretches became a real signature move.

It's not that I didn't know the signs of haemorrhage – every six-year-old knows those from the symptoms jingle.

> A little boy in brands unversed,
> wanted to be big so bad he burst,
> a vessel and blood dispersed.
> Limb's gone dead,
> Lose the thread,
> Words unsaid,
> Reeling head.
> Now he's brand endorsed.
> With all the words rehearsed.

Little kids join hands in a circle to chant it and act out the symptoms – paralysis in the right arm, confusion, impaired speech and dizziness. They all fall down on the word 'head' and leap up again on 'rehearsed'. The day I found Dad in the silo after school, the jingle was running through my head like the music of an ice-cream truck carried on a cold dark night. It was what made me feel sure that he'd had another brain haemorrhage. He had collapsed and I was afraid he wouldn't be bouncing back up again like a kid.

He was lying among a whole shelf of scattered books that he must have pulled with him as he fell. One volume was spread open under his chin. He pinned it to his ribs with his left hand pressing against the binding. He tried to speak but I couldn't understand him. He was a small crumpled note among a grandeur of words. Next to the papery pallor of his face, the leather cover had the oiled, taut look of a wrestler sitting on his chest. When I tried to take it from him so I could help him up, he resisted, making strange noises and pushing the book at me, not letting me put it aside. Only when I opened my hazmat suit and slipped it under my shirt did he sink back into the editions around him.

'Does it hurt?' I asked him. He shook his head but the movement was a grating of gears.

Running up and down the aisles trying to find the book trolley, I felt the leather hide against the skin at the hollow above my hip brushing squid ink into the hollow of my palate. Quickly, a glaze of my sweat started forming on the book's skin, dissolving the salty ink. I thought about the Tigris turning black with the words of the books of Baghdad's House of Wisdom. The Mongols sacked the city in 1258 and emptied the libraries into the river. I had read about that here, in the silo. Now, as if I were on that riverbank, it was all being swept away from me. I couldn't staunch the flow – the shelves of writing leaching out of my life, the language bleeding out of my father's brain, my own haemorrhage.

Getting Dad onto the trolley was difficult. Then I still had to wheel him out the airlock and strip off his hazmat suit before laying him on the floor of his office and calling for help. I needed the paramedics to believe that he had collapsed there rather than in the silo. It was safer for both us and the books. I even went back and hurriedly re-stacked the fallen volumes on the shelf. If Dad didn't get better, I would never be able to return, but at least if the corporates had no reason to believe the books had been touched, they wouldn't think it necessary to destroy them.

When we arrived in the ambulance, Mother had already been called to the hospital to begin the admissions process. Hospitals and banks all look the same: glassed-in clerks guard the assets against the desperate and undeserving. As a distant voice hissed through the microphone, Mother became shrill: 'You're telling me, plus-sizers. I warn you it's not pretty when I get my panties in a twist.' I went over to her, took the plastic ticket from her hand and read, 'Patient number 000473278RTY: Excluded from care due to high-risk lifestyle'. The paramedics had initially wheeled Dad over to the admissions gate but he had been moved aside to the waiting bay with a couple of other stretchers.

Ten minutes later, a doctor came out to meet Mother and led her to a side office. I followed. He waved Mother to a chair but had started speaking before she was even seated. He didn't introduce himself. 'Our records indicate that for a period of three years now, the patient has failed to undergo the required six-monthly post-CVA angiograms, cognitive, psychological and acculturation testing. Furthermore his working environment is rated category five for fungal hazards and he has no brand benefactor. This high-risk lifestyle that encourages pathogenesis is considered a refusal of treatment.'

All that EmPath medical LipService coiled around Mother, deflating her pneumatic curves and making her eyes bulge instead. I saw that she wasn't going to say anything. But the doctor had to be told that the repository has strict health and safety measures – hazmat suits and airlock access. Even if, like everyone else, he believed books caused librarian's lung, I had to convince him of that at least. I began to calibrate a medical defence regarding the repository's lower respiratory risks compared to open-plan offices. It was in a report I had read from years ago when the silos were converted. Then I remembered I couldn't tell him that – he would know I had read it in the repository. I had to slow down, carefully pull a stick from the pile without disturbing the sleeping logs.

Glancing up, I noticed that the doctor was already standing at the door, saying to Mother, 'Your brand status entitles you to use a departure lounge. Here's the access card for 15B.' Then he was gone. I had become so careful about not saying the wrong thing that I had said nothing.

Mother looked as if a waxing strip had been ripped from her skin. 'Oh, oh this is too body shaming. How could he leave me with such a visible panty line? I don't think I can … I must change into something more demure.' She left and I went back to the shuttered clerks to ask to speak to the doctor again. The only response was a finger tapping at a notice posted in the window: 'Patient prognosis and therapeutics are discussed with haemorrh-aged next of kin only. Visitors sign in at entrance 3.' A phonograph voice said 'No LipService patch, no debate.'

Dad was going to die because I had been mute at the moment that mattered most. He had given me those years sitting reading, seeing language leap like static electricity. But when I needed words to ensnare a doctor, it was my tongue that was tied. I failed him. My fists flew at the window with the headlong certainty of beetles that they could get through to the other side. The clerk pressed an alarm and pulled down the blind. I was sobbing so hard that I couldn't speak. A guard came and dragged me off to the Departure Lounge where Dad's stretcher had already been moved.

I tried to tell him that I was sorry I had let him down. He probably didn't understand what I was saying. They had given him painkillers and he slipped in and out of consciousness, a cat following the sunlight on its tour of a room. I climbed onto the stretcher next to him, still snuffling. With his good left hand, he patted the slight bulge on my belly that was the leather-bound volume and smiled with the left half of his face. The book's skin and mine had been pursed together for long enough that it no longer felt different from the jostling of my thighs.

An orderly woke me when he came to take the body away. I went to wait in the lobby for Mother. Looking up from my chair, I saw a black satin dinner jacket that parted to reveal the sorrowing underside of a breast. The band of black velvet blooms on her head and the tenebrous netting extending to just over the tip of her nose made her lips glow like a red light in a window. She looked beautiful and pointless. 'I'm ready to see him now,' she said. I told her that he was already gone.

'But he would've been so tickled to see me as a Frisson Froufrou angel of death.' She turned around to reveal a pair of black-feathered wings.

It took a long time after Dad's death before I could confront the book. It squatted across from me, a mutilated body that was closing in on me without having to move. In queasy sympathy, I imagined my own hide outfitting a book and yet still being able to taste the cloth and board binding of neighbouring volumes on a shelf, or sweaty palms on my back. It was like the compulsion to prod at a dead bird in a gutter with a stick and see its neck flop. I reached out my hand and with a fingertip took a swab of the squiddy leather. My mouth was a seashell carrying echoes of the ocean. That salty marine cleanness can turn so suddenly into the stink of docks. I wasn't even sure which one was truer of the book. I wanted Dad to explain it to me. I wanted Dad. But Dad was gone. There was only Eda-Lyn.

I picked it up again and noticed that instead of a smooth wall of pages, the fore edge had crenellations, with some of the pages sunk deep and others protruding. As my thumb rode over the notches, fanning the pages, the changing fillips of stiff, thick pages and thin, lispy ones sounded like pins and tumblers aligning in a lock. Whirring past on the carousel of pages were titles and names I knew – *The Emperor's New Clothes,* Edward Lear and Kafka. I saw what Dad had done and gave a little gasp of music-box delight. It reminded me of the patchwork book I'd made from the dressing-up clothes, because it was also stitched together from pieces of other works. The original anatomical treatise was gone and in its place was something created just for me. Stories I could keep now that I couldn't go back to the repository. I didn't recognise all the names on the page headers. He had kept things for this moment.

After the flyleaf was a text called *The Fork in the Medicine Tree.* It was a history of medical practice starting from the Middle Ages. The thought of doctors – and of the one who considered my father undeserving of his attentions – tangled impotence and rage in me, like laundry in a spin cycle. When I stilled the throes, I realised that it was just too prescient – as if Dad knew he would be refused care, knew that I needed to understand the men with knives who would slide fingers into my deep, dark crevices when I came of haemorrhage.

The 1163 Council of Tours prohibited clerical physicians from performing any treatment that shed blood. The scalpel's cunning, dentistry and bloodletting were trades for barbers, bath-keepers and sow-gelders. Work for calloused hands. The physician trained as a scholar, examining books, not bodies. Next to this passage, Dad had written in the margin 'copywriters & doctors' – the two powers behind the patch, the two professions that held our tongues.

I read how the power of the church weakened in the Renaissance, and artists began dissecting bodies. Battlefield surgeons followed and gained market share as clerical physicians failed to deliver on their brand promise – to alleviate suffering and heal. The men of letters had to admit the need for the bloody skill of dissection. As for the surgeons, they sought professional prestige and recognition (a quaint way of saying they wanted to brand up to the premium segment) by pursuing book learning and publishing their anatomical findings. Both realised that to capture the market they must have authority over the word and the meat. It's much the same today.

Now it's the words, the books, that are in short supply, but then it was apparently the pounds of flesh. Only convicted murderers could be dissected after hanging, as further punishment for their crimes, and there were never enough of these for medical research and clinical instruction. Instead, the poor who died in the almshouses and cadavers stolen from graves by resurrectionists provided the matter for the making of medical men.

I wondered what Eda-Lyn's relative, the bearer of pork products, had done upon discovering that her corpse had disappeared. The family member was probably about as successful in reclaiming her body from the doctor as I was in getting modern practitioners to care for my father. Maybe Dad never believed that I could convince the doctor of anything after all. Now, just about everyone's body lands on the autopsy table, and fatal second haemorrhages are automatically assigned for post-mortem. Those who pass on weak genetic material must pay off their debts to future society by contributing to the advance of neuroscience.

Concluding with the nineteenth century, *The Fork in the Medicine Tree* describes how doctors' command of scholarly language and a steady scalpel hand came together in books bound in human skin. It was something of a professional vogue. Eda-Lyn was not an exception, then. What's more, the finely worked binding civilised the doctor's 'curing' of the sick: leather has its place in the library, study and museum. And of course, the book had ended up in Dr Ungar Sever's collection – the man whose LipService prescription fixes our broken words. I was unsure what I should be more afraid of – the copywriter and doctor castes, or their upmanship as they try to steal each others' trade secrets.

I thought about Eda-Lyn, who was so hungry and had become a thesis on ravenous worms. I realised that when I went into hospital, I would come out as a leaflet for electric toothbrushes or shoe polish. I traced with a finger over the letters of Dad's note in the margin – I wanted to revive the movement of his hand and for it to offer reassurance. But it was like rolling over a mattress worn out by someone else. Now that the body was gone, the hollows were hard and empty.

The last clump of pages in the book was the story of Echo and Narcissus from the *Metamorphoses*. I had read it to Dad; he liked to hear it declaimed, the parable of our time. If I could find a place where no one would hear me, I would record myself reading it so that I could still hear it out loud after the rupture.

Ovid writes that Juno punished Echo for chattering to her on the mountainside and giving the other nymphs who had entwined their limbs with Jupiter a chance to escape. The goddess says, 'I shall curtail the powers of that tongue which has tricked me: you will have only the briefest possible use of your voice.' From then on, Echo could only repeat the last words another had spoken – like anyone come of haemorrh-age. I often wondered what the nymph talked about to Juno. She must've had words like constellations.

When she sees beautiful Narcissus who 'was driving timid deer into his nets' (that says everything about him), she falls in love with him. I imagine Narcissus as looking like the male model in the Ravish pour Homme cologne ad. His perfectly muscled arms are in the press-up position and he looks down into a dark pool. A perfectly blonde helix hovers over his forehead, suggesting flawless genetic material. The next scene when Echo finds Narcissus alone one day was Dad's favourite.

> The boy, by chance, had wandered away from his faithful band of comrades and he called out: 'Is there anybody here?' Echo answered: 'Here!' Narcissus stood still in astonishment, looking around in every direction, and cried at the pitch of his voice: 'Come!' As he called, she called in reply. He looked behind him and when no one appeared, cried again: 'Why are you avoiding me?' But all he heard were his own words echoed back. Still he persisted, deceived by what he took to be another's voice, and said, 'Come here, and let us meet!' Echo answered: 'Let us meet!' Never again would she reply more willingly to any sound.

It's a monologue that forks into a dialogue. There is Echo with her Narcissus patch and, despite her second-hand speech, she seldom means what he does. The same words become new. I always paused then in my reading, paused over the possibility. And we knew what happens next. She runs to embrace him and Narcissus rejects her. Brands can't reciprocate, they can only gaze spellbound at their own image reflected in a pool. Echo withdrew to lonely caves and withered away. Her bones turned to stone and only her voice remained.

Afterwards, Dad and I would sit still for a moment as my last words reverberated in the silo. Neither Juno nor the rebuff of that fragrance pin-up could silence her.

Eda-Lyn and Echo. Two disembodied voices that keep on speaking, but not their own words. LipServants in perpetuity.

I finished rereading the story but there were still a few pages left. The story of Echo and Narcissus had been pasted in a second time. It made no sense until I got to lines 455–482. Pressed between pages were drops of blood, red dandelions crushed in the moment that the seeds broke away. Dad's nose bled when the aneurysm ruptured. I could see why. The stroke had happened when he was working on these pages. Blacking out many of the printed words and leaving only a chosen few, Dad wrote something that defied LipService. He found a way to echo off Ovid and it shorted his neural circuits.

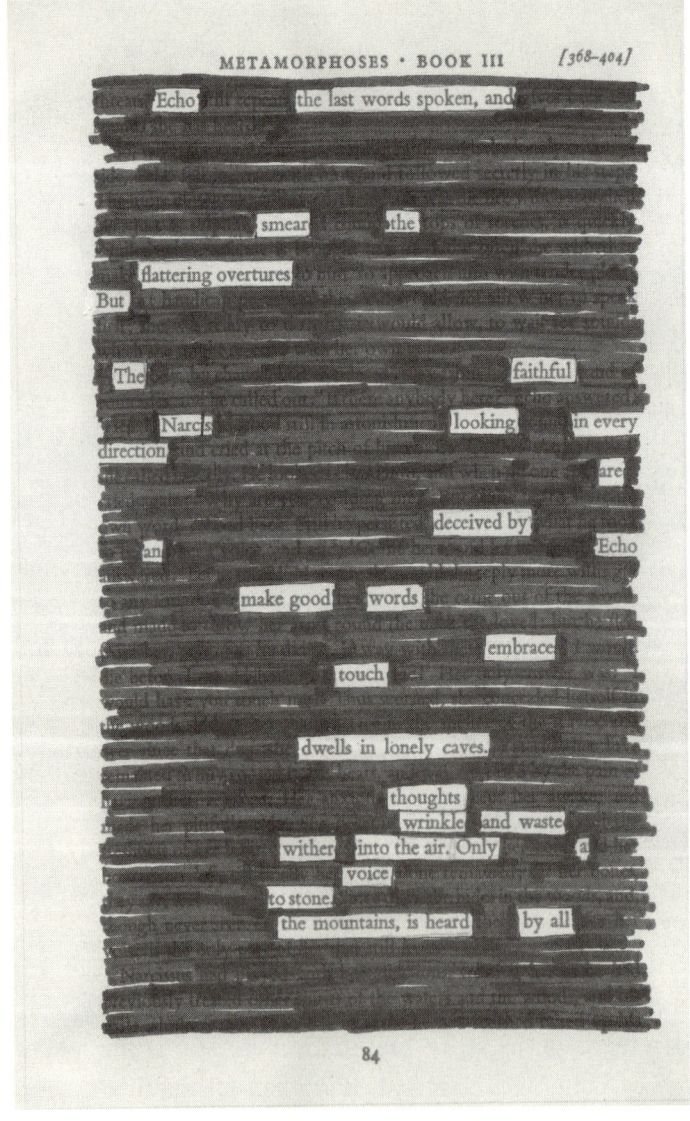

I had cut a piece from Dad's shirt before they took his body away. I wrote out his Echo on it, just as I used to write tastures years ago in my patchwork book made of fabric squares from the dressing-up box. 'Touch dwells in lonely caves.' Lonely caves like the one the tongue sleeps in? Did he taste textures too? Eda-Lyn had made this book an inescapably tangible object – a corporeal corpus.

LipServant

6

You are petering out. The ballpoint rolls on but the ink is stuttering into a Morse code of dots and dashes. This morning as I stepped into the shower, I glimpsed the LipService patch on my shoulder in the mirror. The Dermaluxe paint logo has paled so that the stylised paintbrush looks like the handprint of a prehistoric hunter on a cave wall. That means You don't have much time left. My cells have almost completely metabolised You. I rush into the spaces You are receding from. My lungs rustle with the wind of prohibited words and I start to think I am on the brink of saying something – speaking the unspeakable. Then it's lost. And no sound comes out at all except for a clicking at the back of my throat like the phone being put down.

The Dermaluxe patch slurps at my skin as I peel it off. It's a sound that always summons the memory of the nurse with a face the texture of roughened polystyrene. Every third day at the hospital, she used to stand in the middle of the ward. 'Strip, double over, dispatch,' she would say in an alarm-clock voice, and everyone submissively removed their LipService patch, folded it in half and dropped it in the medical waste container she carried to each bed. I always wanted to gloat at the thought of You stripped, doubled over and finally dispatched. But it was a tartrazine pleasure, a yellow deception. I only had to look at the nurse for my swagger to crumple into a cringe. She was nothing but an intricate plumbing system that gushed LipService. The words passed through her with no resistance. Open the tap and she gurgled away. Is this what becomes of us?

Walking between the beds, nurse continued the catechism: 'Flatlining transdermals is contraindicated. Deliberately depleting LipService to the point of brand blackout is a punishable offence.

Repatching in after brand blackout is likely to induce ...' a jolt – that's what I call it. It's the price for watching when You turn your back to exit.

I wish I were able to put off applying a new patch and slide through a whole day off work without You. I could inhabit my body and mind, not having to share accommodations with You or worry about the impropriety of wandering naked through my interiors. I could sense on my bare skin the air that gives me a flash of nectar nipped from the base of a honeysuckle flower. And You couldn't ruin it with your antiseptic odour of disapproval.

But today I need You. In a few hours I meet Mother at the jetty for Archipelago Arcades – I asked her a week ago to come with me, just hours after I'd left the coffee shop. There, two people ahead of me in the queue was a girl aflutter with labels that were a dozen perfectly placed bets on cool. Even her sunglasses had a jewelled Solar Flair tag that dangled off one arm. As she turned from the counter with her latte, she ran her fingers voluptuously across its top, continuing to talk to her companion. I heard her say 'Formica's oyster-licking greediness.' I turned to her to retort, 'No it's not, it's far more like tanniny black tea.' But I stopped short, all the air sucked out of me. For a moment, there was zero gravity in my head and cogitations floated disconnectedly by. Then I inhaled, things dropped back into place, and I ran after her.

Her LipService brand – I had to know what she was patched into. It was a touch-taste hookup, wasn't it? Did things have tasture for her, too? No, it had to have been copywritten. Her tone made it sound like a product benefit. She wasn't far up the street, and, as I came up behind her, I saw the transdermal on the nape of her neck below the studied carelessness of a messy updo. The logo was Eternal Flame.

I tear open the foil pocket of a new LipService patch. The jagged opening cuts across the Pac-Man-ish head of the Spruce oral-hygiene gum mascot whose jaws are always working, consuming. It's bargain-bin LipService with last season's expressions – the worst thing for Archipelago Arcades. I don't have the money to get anything better now; I've put everything aside for Eternal Flame. I was counting on the Dermaluxe patch lasting through today. Removing the backing from the adhesive, I brace for the Spruce transdermal's contact with skin and the rancid oil slick to wash up on my tongue's shores. Then I wait for your return.

I know your approach by a prickling on the scalp, that feeling of being watched. Every sense is trained on the presence over my shoulder. Then the jolt hits, like walking into a door. The disorientation makes me angry. An imbecile rage that wants to beat at the object that put itself in my way. There's an incessant chatting, chiding coming from a person I can't locate. I want her to be quiet. I can't think. The voice is in my ear. I flail about, hoping to drive her away, and yell, 'Shut up, shut the fuck up!' but instead hear 'Don't let your tongue wag if it makes others gag'.

You're back, all tarted up in your Spruce gum finery. The sudden spike in drug- and electro-stimulation makes You babble. Fragments of Spruce LipService explode like a grotesque bubble of gum, sticking to my eyebrows and hair: 'Are you a breath of fresh air? Goodbye halitosis neuroses! Don't chew the fat, chew to be thin.'

I'm contorting Mother's leather purse that I always use to earth me when the LipService current strikes. The suede has a tasture that I keep returning to. I release my grip and allow my fingers to masticate the seaweedy hide. Mother inherited it from a great aunt and doesn't know I've taken it. She hardly ever uses it and I always hoped she would let me have it. But Mother wants me to covet things of Selkie and Hyde. She wants me to be You.

Mother's bosom holds silicone hopes; they're only natural. When I asked her to come with me to buy an Eternal Flame patch – a gilt-edged LipService brand – what had sagged swelled once again. At last, her daughter was demonstrating the right buyological urges. Of course, she would be delighted to help me find myself with a premium brand – even if it wasn't Frisson Froufrou. *Remember, darling, the key to coming into your own is owning.* For me to now arrive speaking Spruce – a corner-store LipService brand with all the cachet of stale chocolate bars – smacks of insincerity, of subvertising. Yes, I am a shift worker but I should know that an aspirational consumer always trades up. When will I learn that success is nothing if not its trappings?

I am a bad daughter. Even my sweet moments are portents of a downer, a sugar crash. The year I changed schools, Mother was on track to claim her Frisson Froufrou loyalty and service incentive. She was just two years away from augmentation status, when an employee's fleshly form is remade to embody the Frisson Froufrou ideal of firm perkyfection. My defamation of Selkie and the fact that I was moved from the BMG corporation school meant the recapitalisation of her assets was delayed five years.

I can still see Mother standing stripped to the waist in front of the bathroom mirror. Sobbing, she wrenched loose long strips of transparent packaging tape and attempted to truss her bust into shape. The device with the electronic notification had slipped off the vanity onto the floor. I picked it up and read, 'Since you have decided to entrust your child's education to an institution other than the BMG school, we must believe that you no longer embrace the BMG values unreservedly. Such doubts can only affect your ability to act as a brand ambassador …' There was no need to continue. I had done this to her. Will she now suspect me of a more intentional subversion by speaking Spruce when going to buy an Eternal Flame patch?

At least twice a week, I run my finger down the grimy pages of the LipService consumer staples catalogue at the grocery store checkout. Each time, I hold onto my breath and hopes, then tap at a different brand. No words are needed. Cashiers can't be sure whether a customer is in brand blackout or not. Especially as people, like me, who buy consumer staples patches often don't receive a supply of LipService from their employer or much more than a minimum wage. When the money is gone, so is their voice.

In the three years that I've been buying language, I have seldom used the same brand of LipService twice. Somewhere among the rat poison, tinned meat, deodorant and batteries, I keep searching for the version of You that's as gauzy as a muslin teabag and will allow me to seep through. But across all the iterations of You, from the toothpaste smiler to tinfoil tout, I've only ever known You as the kind of woman who would dye her own hair, a coupon collector and buyer of single-ply toilet paper. We are the charity-store set. You will admit as readily as I that it's worth getting that free Prince LipService patch with every tenth purchase of Prince coffee. Just in case.

To Mother, this is an abject assembly-line existence that terminates in landfill. She's convinced that the Frisson Froufrou life is different – that it's coddled in frothy pink tissue paper scented with geranium. Not that her tissue shroud will protect her from the potato peels and car tyres when she enters the ground. But for a while I trusted in her disdain: it was enough to make the banality of necessity brands seem promising to me. After all, Mother's sentiments are not hers alone but carefully manufactured within a consumer community. All I need is for a copywriter equally contemptuous of the clucking, battery-farmed masses to make a careless slip in the linguistic coding. The words themselves won't be mine but I'll feel the charge of static electricity from rubbing up against them, as I used to when reading in the repository. When I finally say something that sings in me, I will write it on walls, on clothes and on kitchen appliances to remind myself that what I hear in my head is real language, an authentic expression and not just a hallucination.

Each patch I've applied has been an act of faith in language's ability to escape the copywriters' grip. With Dermaluxe paint, I imagined unmoored LipService drift about walls tart to the touch. With Love Bites cat food, I promised myself verbal slippage on the savoury nap of fur coats. Even Spruce was chosen with a hopeless fancy that its tackiness might hide real flavour and texture. So far You have proved unrelenting in pushing product benefits and lifestyle enhancement. Nothing You say deviates from the great corporate project. But the girl with the Eternal Flame patch made me think I was wrong not to have tried the elite brands. Maybe I had misunderstood Mother's distaste for cheap LipService. Perhaps she was right; privilege *is* better.

I stand waiting for Mother on the jetty looking out at the islands that form Archipelago Arcades. With the image of the girl from the coffee shop in mind, I have tried to dress appropriately but I know I lack the insouciance and labels. Being able to pay the high price that premium LipService commands isn't enough; you also have to be the right fit with the brand. The exclusivity of Eternal Flame must be guarded. That's why I need Mother. She's bought their skin serums and eye repair treatment. And what she wears are not merely clothes but regalia, part of a complex courtly code of luxury materialism. Without Mother, I have little hope of getting an Eternal Flame transdermal.

We take a gondola to Beauty Island. It's the only place, aside from the brand's invitation-only events, where you can buy Eternal Flame. The store is a summerhouse fronted by a conservatory that juts onto the lake and is filled with specimens of the plants used in the cellular bioenergetics of skin renewal. Jets of mist periodically dew the orchids, and the stirred air sets the crystal chandeliers to tinkling against the percussive drip-drip of water.

The saleswoman who approaches to greet us is the girl from the coffee shop. Her name badge says Lucretia. With the charm of a bank manager keeping a running mental tally, she assesses the peekaboo lace of Mother's camisole that is a porthole into the plunge of her décolleté and the Frisson Froufrou patch placed like an amulet between her clavicles. Extending a hand to Mother, she says, 'Welcome to the flush of youth. Welcome to the glow of Eternal Flame.'

Her skin has the polished luminousness of rose quartz with the light behind it. I wonder what it would taste like to rest my fingertips on her cheek. She's leading Mother to a divan and I'm being left behind. I have to keep my attention from brushing up against every surface.

They are about to sit when suddenly she turns to look at me. Mother must have just told her that I will be the one using the Eternal Flame LipService. A spasm of distaste, as if stepping on a piece of chewing gum in her designer heels, crosses her face.

She recovers quickly to ask, 'Champagne?'

I smile, shake my head and move towards a particularly curious-looking flower with a throat sac like a marabou stork. Mother told me in the gondola that if I sincerely want this patch and am not just set on humiliating her, I am not to open my frumpy Spruce mouth.

So far Lucretia has said nothing with the surreal quality of 'oyster-licking greediness'. That's OK, she probably doesn't want anyone to know about that, and nor do I.

Right now she is saying, 'You must understand that our reputation rests on fighting free radicals, maintaining firmness and erasing irregularities.' The muscles in her jaw thrash below the immaculate surface of her skin.

'Yes, Frisson Froufrou also aims to give women support …'

'Certain women. Eternal Fame is clinically proven to synthesise covetousness. The concentrated effects produced by extract of mass longing are what make our serums so rejuvenating. We cannot allow any impurities in the formula.'

'Ah, the cups must always be half full for most,' says Mother, settling her shoulders back against the divan. Her camisole shifts to reveal a distinctive salmon broderie anglaise bustier strap with candle cutouts. It was the limited edition Frisson Froufrou and Eternal Flame co-branded vintage-style bullet bra. Only ten were made. I don't know how Mother got hold of one. The twin points of her chest prod at Lucretia, whose cheeks show pricks of red.

Mother continues, 'But a brand must hug a customer base's curves, coax them into shape, teach them to defy gravity. You want them in your training bras from a young age.'

Lucretia smooths her skirt over her knees and rises sharply from her wicker chair opposite the divan to clear the champagne glasses. When she returns, she holds an origami orchid that contains within its marabou throat a LipService patch.

On the gondola, I let Mother's social climbing, her coy stratagem, slip into our watery wake, because all I can think of is that she did it for me. I hug her. I don't say anything, so that You can't ruin the lullaby of custard in my throat while pressed to Mother's cheek. Mother just smiles.

I force myself to wait the mandatory three days until the Spruce hygiene gum patch is low but not flatlined. Strip, double over and dispatch. You slip off my skin. The Eternal Flame patch is powder-puff pink and is embossed with an orchid blossom lying in front of a lit candle. The only printing is the gold lettering 'Eternal Flame', and below, in a smaller typeface, 'The glow that never leaves your cheeks'. It's so lovely I can almost understand the appeal of wearing it prominently like an ornament. But it's not just an ornament, it's an insignia of social rank, a statement of identity, and I don't belong. I apply it above my hip. And reach for a marker pen.

I fixate on the words 'Formica's oyster-licking greediness' and put the pen to my left inner arm, preparing to inscribe my skin with its truth. The letters lurch along and I gaze at 'Formula's moisture-locking ingredients'. I don't understand. How did this happen? Flicking mentally back and forth between the two phrases, I realise that they have the same auditory silhouette.

I must have filled in the outline.

You are laughing.

7

For two years, since my Eternal Flame folly, I've spent weekdays sitting behind the window at Lost Property. That's the longest I have kept a job. My rubber-stamp responsibilities are so far removed from the gravitational pull of any corporate identity that no LipService brand is mandated for my working hours.

Sometimes, days pass without anyone approaching my window. Aside from your interruptions, I'm free to think my own thoughts away from the rapid fire of brand triggers. Plus, as I learned when Dad died here, hospital administration believes that people should be separated by sheets of sound-insulating glass like dead slices of brain between slides, all electric connections gone. Although I'm really the one inside the box, it's the people on the outside who appear to flicker across a screen. They are remote, characters on a TV with the sound down. This is how it's possible for the reception clerks at the hospital front line to remain as detached as a weather balloon. The world on mute, even with all the suffering, is faintly ridiculous. In here, it's just You and me locked in our sullen sitcom.

Behind us, on the left, are cartons of clutter forgotten by visitors or patients. Separate containers are dedicated to mobile devices, spectacles, dentures, jewellery, logoed false nails, sweaters and keys. These are the things that the living leave behind as carelessly as hair on a pillow.

The boxes on the right, each labelled with a photo of the deceased and name, if known, are different. Really, these articles are not lost, it's their owners who are lost, who were left behind. They died without a brand tribe, and relatives can't be found. There's seldom anyone who comes to claim these last bodily possessions, which are boxed anyway, just in case. Generally, they hold the same clutter as the other cartons – the same personalia that form the repeating pattern on the wallpaper of human life. Only now the human face, the oil painting that hung for so long in front of the identical drops, has been removed, and the motifs behind it of watch, wallet, hairpiece and jacket appear unnaturally vivid as they profile a negative space alive with absence.

You are compelled by the collection on the left with its artefacts that narrate a soap opera of brands getting in bed with one another, designs undergoing facelifts and flirtations with bright new things. As You like to remind me, 'Our lives are really product stories.' I want to tell You that You're wrong just because it's You. But I can't deny that it's the objects we carry with us that define whether we are rich, desirable and beautiful. And who would I be without the stack of books that I carry like an invisible totem pole in my head? Or the way that I taste objects?

I've heard rumours about personal history videos screened at CEOs' and copywriters' funerals. A series of shots depict a still life in which the deceased's various mobile phones, smart devices and status purchases are successively faded in. These artfully directed videos of branded goods in their various iterations – the deceased's significant others – can move mourners to uncontrollable weeping.

There were no such elaborate solemnities for Dad, not even a memorial service. Mother didn't want his 'final bra-burning moments' advertised. One bleed is a glorious revolution; two is anarchy. I think of Dad a lot here in my cubicle because not much happens. And while it's not the book repository, it is an archive of sorts. The cardboard of the boxed compendiums is plastic coated, and seeing it on the shelves always makes me think, they just had to do that to the pages and we could've still had books. Unless the point was not to have books. Or at least none of the ones from before.

For me, it's the repository on the right that tugs at my sleeve. I imagine that the best cartons can teach me to listen for the nail-clipper noise of beetle jaws, the gnawing destruction at work beneath the triumphant clamour of the marching brands. Insects can fry sophisticated circuitry, paralyse organisational structures and topple our empires of worldly goods. I'm sure the only way to beat LipService is by scurrying along the skirting of corporatised society. The box owners were mostly as outdated as the clothes they wore and the paraphernalia they carried. And the old go unnoticed, as You derisively put it: 'It's planned obsolescence. Leaky creakies are cop-out consumers. We only want the young, the new, the now, the next.' But it's possible that some of them might even have remembered when the LipService code conventions were still being ironed out. If anyone can point me to the bugs in LipService, it must be them. That and the quiet is why I've stayed with this job.

Their things are all around me. I just need to learn to read the correspondences between the objects in a box when I lay them out like a spread of tarot cards on a table. But this personal baggage is cryptic. Take the labels inside the clothes. I sometimes wonder whether they are even brands. In a box with no name for the deceased, there's a jacket with a label at the neck that reads 'Thackwell's, 24 Church Street'. That sounds more like the return address, should Mr Thackwell's jacket go astray. I like to tell myself that this was a custom in an era when a jacket merely 'became' you, unlike now when you become the jacket – slipping on its brand personality with the sleeves. And there's the heavy tweed cloth, worn at the elbows, that isn't used much any more. I let the pink tongue of my finger rasp at the coarse wool streams of warp and weft, drinking in peat smoke and malted alcohol. There's a sense of the man in the flavour of his garments. In the pocket is an old matchbox with a small dead iridescent beetle inside.

The first time I lifted the lid of such a carton, hearing the sound of cardboard clearing its throat before opening wide, was when I took out Dad's shirt and spread it on my bed. There it lay, sunk into itself, withdrawn behind an agitation of creases. I wanted it to be at peace so I folded the arms, right over left across the chest like a dead Egyptian pharaoh, but the cloth only bunched more. Smoothing the worn corduroy pants in long licks of stewed guava, I skidded over pips in the pockets and withdrew a pair of earplugs. On the duvet, the earplugs spooned with a pair of white cotton manuscript gloves that I'd found in the other pocket. I moved his scratched horn-rimmed reading glasses and a small surgical face mask next to them. This collocation of objects portrayed my father as I'd never seen him before – a man who muffled his senses, who closed out the sensual excitement of the material world. Maybe I had misunderstood 'touch dwells in lonely caves'. Maybe he didn't have tastures, or spurned their advances. But having tried to repress them myself, I couldn't believe it was even possible. My father lived between the lines and between the linings of his pockets.

The boxes don't like having their sleep disturbed. When I bump up against the stacks, reaching for one high up, bells jangle in alarm. Each box contains a string of chimes that was hung off the limbs of the corpse for twelve hours in case the person revived. Brand champions and corporate chieftains get 'jingle bells' – electronic chimes with motion sensors that play the brand jingle to soothe the fright of awaking in a mortuary and alert staff to the reawakened.

Really, it's the living who are afraid. Few families get to bury a body. Corpses are almost always awarded to medical science for further research or instruction – 'as the best method to leverage human resources in repayment of debts to society' (so goes the catechism) – especially after a second haemorrhage like Dad had. The bereaved murmur that if it's doctors who are so eager to claim our raw materials, should we trust them to decide whether or not someone has truly died? Those declared dead simply vanish as completely as a fire breather's exhalation, leaving nothing, not even ashes. The only remains are a tinkling string and box of folded clothes and oddments.

The tradition is to remove the chimes' tongues – to hush them. With Dad's bells it should've been Mother who com-muted the clappers, but she'd had her nails freshly manicured and logoed so she turned them over to me. I twisted and snapped, my mettle fatigued. Eventually it occurred to me that my mechanical movements were no different from the repetitive stresses of self-censorship. I left the last bell intact, the last tongue tinging.

More boxes arrive for storage. I always have to look inside, even if I face your jeers at my pursuit of cast-offs and hand-me-downs. Sometimes the collection inside is so unremittingly ordinary, I doubt if it even belonged to an individual and not a buyer persona. This brings on the playground chant of 'poor, obscure, no allure' from You. But the contents of one of the new arrivals is a curious miscegenation. Although barely worn – I catch that never-been-washed, new-fabric smell – the clothes are clearly by brands with virtually no share of mind. And yet, unfranchised consumers would never hack out labels as had been done here, leaving a hole in the fabric at the neck of the hoodie. All other identification is also missing. There's no wallet, no bank or credit cards, only a cheap billfold with a couple of grubby notes. The box label says: 'Male, age approx 37, cause of death: impact by tram.'

But any residue of the idea that this might be a member of the beetling class is utterly wiped away, into a handkerchief – a handkerchief of golden spider silk. Textiles made from the filament of *Nephila madagascariensis* fit only the pockets of the corporocrats – not polyester plebeians. Either this guy was a thief or he had counterfitted himself out as something he wasn't. As I touch the handkerchief, I briefly forget all about male, age 37.

For a moment, You and I are planets in conjunction. The fabric tastes beatific – of honey, no, saffron-infused honey. We stand for a long time letting the gold enhalo us. It coos to us with your voice: 'We know how to appreciate it. We should take it.' No. This is a box that someone will come for. I don't feel that he's a thief. Not even thieves cut holes in their clothes – only someone who considers such wardrobe items purely disposable could be so careless. You howl with disappointment and I feel it.

Packing the things back into the carton, I notice that the Harrington jacket is heavier on one side. I check the pockets again – empty. I frisk the jacket. There's something flat trapped in the right side. The lining has been torn away to create a pouch. Inside, the owner stowed a flexible tablet computer.

It takes me a while to switch it on because it's so futuristic – probably a prototype. I've never seen one like it. A galaxy glow illuminates a document on screen headed *Client brand: Smite-M insecticide*. Below that, *Project: LipService flanking materials – brand narrative; Copywriter: Declamartiste*; and a date.

Copywriter codenames supposedly protect the programmers' identities and limit the risk of corporate espionage, but are ultimately just another way to a put a brand face on their work. While I was still at school, the Great Dictator had name recognition that began to challenge even LipService itself – although no one knew who he or she really was. Over weekends, kids would beg their parents to buy and apply Disport patches, which shouted 'Verbal stylings by the Great Dictator' from a yellow starburst, so that on Monday they could dumbfound their friends by repeating snow sports LipService drift along the lines of 'smoking the halfpipe'. Then GD just dropped out of speech, with only a vague mention in an uncharacteristically subdued press release: 'The Great Dictator is heading off-piste onto fresh powder.' Mother said the copywriter 'had to be corseted. GD got too big for her brand, letting it disappear between the rolls of blabber. Control briefs were required.' Mother is very canny about that kind of thing.

The name Declamartiste doesn't mean anything to me, but then again no individual copywriters have generated anything like the chatter around Great Dictator. From what Mother said, I suppose there was probably an intervention to ensure it never happens again. Even if he was no GD, I think 'male, age approx 37' *was* Declamartiste – a real active copywriter, not just a burnt-out one turned headmaster, cut off from the supply of unprogrammed LipService.

I look at the clothing in the box, which recently rose and fell to the rhythm of free speech. I want that. And why can't I have it – what copywriters have? And the more I want it, the more I despise them for denying it to me. Prying into the jacket's polyester, I try to reprise the last traces of that language from the creases, only it's not words that gush into my mouth. The camel's-milk tasture neutralises the heartburning hate enough for me to wonder again what a copywriter was doing wearing abused polyester and without the identification that would've ensured his bodily possessions a more fitting afterlife than this box.

I start reading the document on the screen, hoping to find the answer there. It appears to be the copywriter's notes on adapting Kafka's story *The Metamorphosis* into a brand narrative for the insecticide Smite-M.

Selling LipService

Purchasing message key points
- Insecticide is a necessity for household hygiene and health.
- The good consumer is molested by pests (it's a scourge, they're among us everywhere!) intent on our resources, happiness.
- Pesticides aren't dangerous when used as indicated.

Surprisingly, Declamartiste quotes passages from the original and details their place in his plans for the Smite-M version.

> One morning, when Gregor Samsa woke from troubled dreams, he found himself transformed in his bed into a horrible vermin.

A family tragedy – eldest son (Gregor Samsa) suddenly transformed into a horrible vermin. What has he done to deserve this fate? Well, as the very opposite of a fire-brand travelling salesman (boss says, 'Your turnover has been very unsatisfactory of late') for a textiles company, his lukewormery is truly contemptible:

> 'If I didn't have my parents to think about I'd have given in my notice a long time ago, I'd have gone up to the boss and told him just what I think, tell him everything I would, let him know just what I feel. He'd fall right off his desk!' (thank our lucky brain scars there's LipService to prevent such mewly pukey talk!)

Gregor literally becomes (allegory!) the brand parasite that he is. Story told from perspective of bleeding-heart li'l sis Grete who cares for creepy crawler through misguided sense of kinship, even though it nauseates her. Big mistake.

> No sooner had she come in than she would quickly close the door as a precaution so that no one would have to suffer the view into Gregor's room, then she would go straight to the window and pull it hurriedly open almost as if she were suffocating. Even if it was cold, she would stay at the window breathing deeply for a while.

She still found his appearance unbearable and would continue to do so, she ... even had to overcome the urge to flee when she saw the little bit of him that protruded from under the couch.

Character arc – sis must learn that good consumers have zero in common with evil arthropods. We must guard our resources against them. Only the fittest survive (note how long it takes the bug to die, even without eating and with a festering apple in its back – months). Reason for instinctive gut churning is insects are sickening, cause disease. In final epiphany sis says to parents, 'It'll be the death of both of you, I can see it coming ... it's got to go.' This is what vermin do – repulsive infiltrators. Terminate with extreme prejudice or they will force us from our homes, our food. Great speech by li'l sis:

> You've got to get rid of the idea that it's Gregor. We've only harmed ourselves by believing it for so long. How can that be Gregor? If it were Gregor he would've seen long ago that it's not possible for human beings to live with an animal like that and he would've gone of his own free will. We wouldn't have a brother any more, but then, we could carry on with our lives and remember him with respect. As it is this animal is persecuting us, it's driven out our tenants, it obviously wants to take over the whole flat and force us to sleep on the streets.

Mother and father paralysed. They do nothing – irresponsible attitude that allows pest to spread misery. Ineffectual father attempts to repulse home invader with ridiculous foot stamping, newspaper waving and later pelting bug with apples.

> Gregor's father seized the chief clerk's stick in his right hand ... picked up a large newspaper from the table with his left, and used them to drive Gregor back into his room, stamping his foot at him as he went.

> ... lightly tossed, something flew down and rolled in front of him. It was an apple; then another one immediately flew at him ... father had decided to bombard him. He had filled his pockets with fruit from the bowl on the sideboard and now, without even taking the time for careful aim, threw one apple after another.
>
> Grete does only reasonable thing. Buys can of Smite-M. Bug dies gassed in chamber. Cloud lifts, family decides to have day out at mall together for the first time in months. Mr and Mrs Samsa realise daughter will haemorrhage soon. She's become a consumer in her own right, brand empowered. A happy ending.

'Wow, that's adding value, morally incentivising the purchase of Smite-M.' You're breathless with admiration. 'So transformational! Turning that mopey, sad-sack story into the coming of haemorrhage of Grete. And it works on so many levels – because brand perfunctionaries really are like bugs with their heads pushed low to the ground by their big hunched backs.' I'm trying to shut out your frothy effusions, to tell myself not to let Declamartiste's impresario performance stop my eyes adjusting to the shapes in its darkness. I must think. 'And the chance to see how a copywriter's mind works – even you've got to be excited about that, Frith,' You jubilate.

Concentrate. Kafka's *Metamorphosis* is one of the stories in the human book Dad gave me, but Declamartiste would've had to go to the book repository to get a copy of it. That means the silo shelves are probably still intact. It's five years since I left them with Dad, and I feel a stupid kiss-planting gratitude to the copywriter for letting me know that they're all still there waiting, the titles read and unread.

Once the realisation has settled and sedimented, I reread the copywriter's notes. It isn't just the gleeful savagery that keeps knifing me. I know that Smite-M also sponsors advergames where players build up arsenals of aerosol chemical weapons (nerve gas, antifeedants, growth regulators) of varying effectiveness on a range of monster mutant insects. Fire the right spray at the right bug and you get to watch it die in gory detail. So that was probably to be expected. But Declamartiste's horror at poor Gregor's ability to survive so long without consuming – I think that's why he relishes Gregor's death so much. Nothing is more horrible than a failure to consume. He expresses the same disgust when the parents do nothing (what he means is buy nothing) and the family is only rehabilitated by going to the mall. It's also why You're cheering. This is your credo, too.

I still don't know why a copywriter died badly dressed, run over in a shabby neighbourhood. Swiping over to the next page, there is only a heading: 'Covert market research observations: Fumigation of apartment block at 6 Tenth Street'.

I picture Declamartiste, his skin prickling inside the polyester jacket and pants, wondering whether he dares clutch the golden handkerchief to his nose. Has he caught a whiff of the chloropicrin released as a warning before the odourless fumigant, or is it just the rank file milling about? The tented building looks like a giant circus top. And outside it, he is surrounded by *blue-collar true squalor*. He notices that they gesture and grimace a lot when they talk, throwing themselves bodily into a farce of expression. He must study them like traffic patterns worn into the supermarket floor, marking the migratory movements of the herd.

'Imagining the copywriter putting on perfumed airs, eh Frith? You're always so sure they're looking down their nose jobs at everyone else. But who creates equal optimism through LipService, so that all adults keep their spirits up with a cheery turn of brand praise?'

And who goes spying on us in our neighbourhoods because they can't trust a word of our chipper chatter – having scripted it themselves?

'"Spying", that's so passé. It's observational market research – gaining a better understanding of target market behaviours and needs to improve products.'

Or to invent new jiggery-pokery to sell the same old stuff. I put the OLED panel back into the jacket and close the box. But

Declamartiste has already escaped and is cutting a caper across my mental stage.

It's about a week since I excavated Declamartiste's carton, and I see a man approaching my window. He moves like an astronaut, as if trying to avoid contact with his cheap synthetic clothes. As he inserts a finger to scratch underneath his woollen beanie, I notice what is clearly the scabbing of a hair transplant. Immediately, I know who he is – one of them.

I want him to speak, to hear him use unbranded LipService and loop-the-loop language as only a copywriter can.

'In-hale and hearty with Suck-o-Matic's clean-air design.'

A vacuum cleaner greeting? Disappointing, but I probably should've expected it as part of the whole 'average consumer' act. I imagine him practising it in front of the bathroom mirror. When it's not neurally programmed, LipService drift doesn't come naturally. It didn't to me before I haemorrhaged and I wonder whether he can sustain the brand suck-up. I smile but leave him to continue.

'I've come to make a clean sweep of my brother's remains.'

'It leaves a gap in your smile when one of your set is suddenly pulled,' I say because I'm patched into Big Grin's toothpaste – not the best brand for condolences. I don't know if Declamartiste really was his brother. I doubt it. He's probably just had the paperwork forged so that he can claim the box as a family member and get back that high-tech panel and the Smite-M adaptation. Maybe he won't have thought of preparing to make an emotive brand pitch.

'Yes, we miss him terribly. So gifted.' Brusque, like the short, sharp jerk of pulling legs off a spider. I had almost forgotten how cutting a statement without brand alerts could be, and the surprise shows on my face. He must've resented Declamartiste. Were they rivals? I had unintentionally antagonised him. Corporates don't like copywriters to be outed in public – it distracts from the message and reminds shoppers of what they can't buy into. Someone always has to pay for such indiscretions.

I try to recover my brand face. 'You know the drill, there are holes to fill. Records, please.'

He pushes the documentation for the release of the box through the slot under the glass of my window. I check through it, rubber-stamping where appropriate, and slide the box out a door in the wall next to my window.

The copywriter turns and is gone before I can say anything else. I'll miss having Declamartiste on the shelf.

8

Today, I need to wear You like a fast-food mascot costume, to shrink myself into insignificance within your cartoon cranium. Until now, all my post-CVA testing has been to establish baselines. But today when I go for the battery of tests – an assault of electrodes, straps, questions and psychological probing – I'll be captured. My results entered for analysis in the cohort database. When their contrast agent shines his flashlight around the inside of my skull, my thoughts must retreat, squirming grubs before the brightness. All that can be allowed to show up on the fMRI is the great hollowness of your bobble head. I can't allow the doctors to see the neural fire of insurgency that must go off every time I speak LipService. But what if in allowing You and your brandstanding full executive powers, I can no longer reclaim myself? What if I'm exiled forever from the control room and can only watch as You operate me like an animatronic figure in a theme park for the rest of my life?

A few weeks ago, in the hospital canteen, a medical intern was brag-swaggering about 'improved prediction of buying behaviour based on fMRI readings of increased activity in the medial prefrontal cortex'. He was momentarily reduced to a pile of crumpled clothes when the pretty nurse he was with couldn't see why this was such a big deal. When he explained that even those who sincerely intend to purchase a product or change their buying behaviour in the future often don't go through with it, she became far more interested in the fact that people don't know their own minds than in his breakthrough. She was toy-ploying with him. I don't like the canteen much, but sitting quietly and eating or very slowly sipping tea is essential for staying ahead of the neuromarketing swerve. I call it reconloitering – one of the great advantages of working at the hospital. That's how I know I need You to tap-dance across my prefrontal cortex in a show of consumer enthusiasm.

After days of indecision, I've chosen to patch into a supermarket multivitamin – 'Multipill: You times ten.' Yes, I know I shouldn't be taken in by the slogan and that it probably won't make You any different to what You usually are. But my reasons are good. No tactile or gustatory product benefits (it's advertised as having 'swift-swallow tasteless capsule technology'). Therefore, no LipService drift to threaten dangerous brushes with tastures. It's impossible to know what they would do if they discovered that my touch-taste tangles survived the haemorrhage. Trying to guess, my imagination goes into free fall – brain surgery, reconditioning therapy, chemical correctives? Multipill is also a choice that shows I care about my health but am not such a social climber as to go for a designer supplement cocktail.

I'm met by a Dr Bromide rather than the usual brain hacks who conduct standard testing. The presence of the doctor means they have found something in the baseline data. Only high-value research subjects – influentials, ebrandgelists, celebrities or anomalies – are flagged for qualitative projects run by doctors, rather than broad quantitative capture. There's no other reason to be interested in me. I don't have the status quo-tient. I desperately start trying to reel in my nerves, recoil the fibres of feeling deep between the organs and leave my skin dead and dumb. Instead the anxiety sends me into a fizz like a snail sprinkled with salt.

I'm taken for the fMRI first. My time inside the tunnel starts as usual with watching a series of product images and new TV commercials. I focus on letting You do the thinking. It's all quite ordinary until an ad comes on for an antiseptic showing a mother cleaning the graze on a kid's knee with a cotton wool swab. At that moment, a tuft of cotton wool is pressed into my hand. I don't hear or see any of the techs approach because of the noise of the magnetic coils and the ad's soundtrack coming through the earphones. The surprise contact almost makes me choke on cheap spirit vinegar. A little while later, the wad is removed from my hand and a rubber ball takes its place – just as a man throws a similar ball for a collie in a dog-biscuit ad. I hate rubber; it burns with chilli agonies down my throat and nose. Even with the cage that closes over my face and the bolsters to keep my head from moving, I've never been claustrophobic inside the machine bore. But as my gullet blisters and irrationality spreads like inflammation, I feel unable to escape, unable to control the stimulus or my response. I realise I'm yelling into the microphone for them to get me out.

One of the techs brings me a glass of water to drink in the consultation room while I wait for Dr Bromide. Lifting the glass, I spill some.

He's already speaking when he comes in: 'I hypothesised increased cortical excitement of the left anterior insula in response to tactile stimulation.' I don't know whether he's addressing me. But there's no one else in the room.

'The results validate this entirely. Influence of media persuasiveness on the subject is, however, inconclusive.' Then I notice him press the button on a voice recorder in his breast pocket. His smile is the kind usually only achieved with a dental retractor.

'It must be apparent by now that we are treating this case involving cross-modal interaction and the corresponding gustatory hallucination.'

He is now definitely talking *to* me but also *about* me – as if I'm not the test subject under discussion. It creates the disquieting sense that the person in the MRI hadn't really been me at all. What if he's making an appeal to You?

'Further investigation of the neurological mechanisms of this syndrome and its potential genetic markers are a scientific imperative. But we can't let the sympathetic nervous response in the MRI adversely affect our efforts by developing into avoidance behaviour.'

I cling sweatily to the words that give me history, continuity and the memory of Dad – genetic markers: 'The ... the tastes are naturally sourced from my father?'

I'd hoped Multipill would be a useful brand in a medical context but somehow, whatever LipService I choose, my words always sound idiotic in my own ears.

'No, via the X chromosome.'

'My mother?' The woman who did nothing when the principal pulled me out of class and the other kids started picking on me. And all the time she knew – experienced tastures herself? Even You are surprised.

'Since social adaptation through brand identification has reduced patient zero's concurrent response to the tactile inducers, our present case is all the more critical for data collection. Patient zero was accordingly instructed under threat of corporate redundancy to prevent research bias due to demand characteristics in the development of the new subject's cross-talk between sensory systems. Now that the subject's neural pathways have been established, patient zero's influence is less of a factor.'

The horror of what he says is a shuddering palsy, a loss of control that it appears I never had. And Mother? I always thought she chose Frisson Froufrou, chose to ignore my off-brand behaviour and its causes. Was that her kindness? To discourage me from the things that would only lead me like a lab rat into Dr Bromide's maze? But what has it helped? The flavours are involuntary and perhaps all the rest of my life was as preprogrammed as LipService.

Is she relieved now that she's losing her taste? One less unwanted jerk and twitch in response to a doctor's reflex hammer?

'Can we continue with the procedure? Need I remind you that failure to cooperate with consumer health research objectives constitutes a refusal of care?' says Dr Bromide.

I stand up on legs that aren't mine and follow him out the door.

A postnasal drip of liver pâté creeps down my throat from the cold moist sponges strapped to my head. They contain electrodes, and the liquid is an electrolyte solution. Stillwell, one of the lab techs assisting Dr Bromide, explains this in a soft voice as he wires me to a small box. Techs are normally aloof, guarding against over-identification with the subject. The fear must be quivering off me – a haze from hot tarmac distorting the horizon. And it's true, I can't see past the mirage, the possibility of pain. Even if Stillwell says, 'Transcranial direct current stimulation is a non-nociceptive procedure.'

After overseeing the placement of the electrodes on my head, Dr Bromide takes Stillwell aside. I can't hear his instructions but the repetitive stabbing of his right index finger into the opposite palm mimics an anaesthetist failing to find the vein and achieve the desired surrender. The tech looks nervous. The door to the lab opens and Dr Bromide abruptly stops needling Stillwell and announces to the room, 'As part of medicorporate cooperation, copywriter Wordini will now administer the prescribed tests.' With that he sweeps out past the copywriter without a greeting or a second glance.

Wordini walks up to where I'm seated, wires dangling off my head, and extends his hand: 'You must be feely Frith. Isn't this exciting?'

I shake his hand limply. Feely Frith – it sounds like a sideshow act.

'And? How do I taste? I'm sweet aren't I – like a cream puff? No, wait. I'm more complex than that ... 1986 Château Lafite Rothschild? An extraordinary vintage.'

I shrug. What does he want from me? To pair him with a pheasant pithivier or pan-fried scallops? Has he forgotten that his work ensures that I probably couldn't say that anyway? All that would come out is some drivel about the nutritive value of omega-3 fish oils. I refuse to answer.

'Come, come – aren't I a linguoso treat? Most people are thrilled to glitz to meet a copywriter.' I can't tell if he's trying to win me over or if he's just a child who wants to see the bear dance and fails to notice the stick and chain. I don't want to perform. I want to crawl into a blanket fort of catatonia and try to decipher the shadows on the walls, but instead I have to come out and play nice. So I say, 'I have no control over the formulation of oral supplements.'

'Ah.' He sounds disappointed. Stillwell makes use of the moment to catch the copywriter's eye and point to his watch. 'Science is always so sure there's nothing to be learned from the consumer arts or conversation,' Wordini snaps.

You've never wanted any part of the tastures – advertsorial deviancy – and You'll not have your personality disordered by such an aberration. You put up a wall between us just as the tech slides a table with cubicle panels in front of me so that I'm boxed in – I can see neither my hands in my lap nor anything ahead or to my sides.

'I call this a little game of tat for titillation. We place some old tat in your hands without you seeing what it is and you name the finger food, how intensely it titillates the taste buds on a scale of one to ten and whether it tattles on the tat,' says Wordini, grinning. 'A *stimulating* divertissement, don't you think?' He really could sell anything. Even having electrodes strapped to your head and not knowing what will happen when the switch is flipped. But the day so far has conditioned me with an animal distrust. I'm not going to lick his hand and let him pat my head. I manage to lift a lip enough to show a courteous fang.

'Our tech Stillwell here is applying a secondary patch to give you a bit of a verbocharge.'

'Is it slow-release preparation?' The words come out before I can think. Wordini chortles with delight. I'd stupidly given him all the leverage he could ask for. Showing that I crave language, want more freedom of speech; he's got me where he wants me.

'Lamentably, no, my little word wanton. It's fast acting but short lived. Specifically developed for research such as this.'

Before the first object – taste of menthol, four out of ten, a glass bottle – reaches my right hand, my left index and middle finger have also had electrodes taped to them.

'Skin conductance response – measuring degree of emotional arousal,' says Stillwell softly and adds, 'Facial coding for complementary data readings on emotional state,' in an embarrassed mumble when he notices me eyeing what is clearly a camera lens set into the back wall of the cubicle.

I can see they intend to empty my contents, upend drawers, toss the mattress. The strewings will all be roughly raked over in the search. For what? I don't know and it hardly matters when there will be nothing left that hasn't been pawed. What happens to people who no longer have any secret things nestled in dark places?

More objects pass across my tongue – cold ham, five out of ten, steel key. Then I suddenly feel a nettling burn at the electrodes on my head. They couldn't have been switched on before. It's only just beginning now. A new flavour forces itself on my hand – pumpernickel bread, eight out of ten, wooden spoon. Hunks of rye lodge unswallowed in my throat. Why is it so strong? But the spoon is already gone and my fingers are splayed open around something new – very dark chocolate, nine out of ten, glazed porcelain teacup. It's such bitterly dark cacao. I don't understand what's happening. Are the tastures turning on me, like in an autoimmune response? The rubber ball is returned to my hand. The intensity is unbearable. My fingers rear back and then retreat inside my sleeves, gasping.

Somewhere behind me, Wordini's voice says, 'Yes, yes, spit it out. But in words please.'

'Chilli, ten out of ten, rubber ball.' I wonder whether I'll even be able to taste anything else.

Still the objects keep pushing forward, crowding in on me with their restaurant-kitchen shouts. There's a dullness to my palate as if it were scalded. The polyester of a sock is still milky but the peculiarly camel smack of it is weak, more a memory. And dry grasses, I feel their keen edges, a hair off a paper cut, but instead of the sharp chlorophylls of raw green peas they're mushy, overcooked, lifeless – two out of ten. And then comes paper. More than the shock that somehow a disease carrier has found its way into the hospital and is being pressed into my hands by the staff is that it has no taste. Nothing at all. Nothing of the soft chickpea hours in the book repository. My mouth hangs open, empty.

'Oh ho, is it a slip of the tongue?' says Wordini's disembodied head, which appears above the cubicle wall, 'Or are you losing your touch? Let's confirm you've no taste for tangibles.' The invisible hand pulls free the paper and butts my fingers with a small smooth pellet – a gel capsule.

'Multipill?'

'A supplement and no fine dining?' insists Wordini.

'Yes.'

I have been taken apart like a transistor radio. I am in pieces, disconnected. This is a show of how deeply they can twist the screwdriver, these engineers of the human parole. How they can strip out my tastures as easily as they blew the circuit breaker of my language. And what am I left with? No real taste, no real food but the equivalent of a nutritional supplement – Multipill.

Stillwell is called over to wheel away the cubicle and remove the electrodes from my fingers and head.

He pats my hand after he has coiled up the creeping cables and says, 'Baseline cortical excitability of the left anterior insula can be enhanced or attenuated by anodal and cathodal transcranial direct stimulation respectively. Apparently, cathodal stimulation reduces the signal-to-noise ratio, producing an elevation in your sensory cross-activation. The reverse occurs with anodal stimulation. But these effects are temporary.'

'Are you sure?'

'Of course, we wouldn't dream of robbing you of your acquired taste, my dear guinea prig,' interrupts Wordini. 'Quite the contrary, together you and I are going to pioneer a marketing fame changer, a new brandiloquence with tongue firmly in chic …'

Stillwell is staring intently at Wordini, trying to signal something. Looking up, the copywriter sees Dr Bromide has returned.

'Attempting to inoculate my research subject against me?' he says.

'Not at all, I'm simply making my pitch, and market forces will prevail,' replies Wordini. 'Should our feely Frith prefer the flavour of a finger in my pie, she would receive a supply of unbranded LipService and remuneration commensurate to her mouth-watering gifts. But I'm sure, Doctor, that you, too, have a compelling offer.'

Still in my seat, I see the wind gusting violently through the doctor's nasal thickets.

'Ethical responsibility cannot be entrusted to the vagaries of market economics. You,' he says pointing at me, 'have an ethical responsibility to the field of neuroscience and the fight against a pandemic of cerebrovascular disease. But since you probably only understand metastasising materialism, I can arrange a cosmetic procedure of your choice.'

They are both looking at me. So are You. Except You can't decide which You want. As for me, I think Bromide can keep his fucking fake tits and cheeks, but unbranded LipService – I want that.

I haven't answered yet, but Stillwell apparently lacks any sense of social timing and has started to present the results of the transcranial simulation trials to Dr Bromide.

His voice is low but clear: 'Preliminary results of facial coding and galvanic skin response track self-reported intensity levels of the gustatory hallucination, correlating with a strong emotional association ... and possibly individuation.'

'Not now!' snaps the doctor, waving him away. Before scuttling off, Stillwell gazes at me with the eyes of a man inside an iron lung, reminding me of the nettling electrodes, the fear and claustrophobia. They make me think he wasn't talking to Dr Bromide at all. After having tapped my calls between touch and taste, he is offering advice. The message is in the word 'individuation'. Tastures are the language of my memories and desires. Who would I be if they were simply more tradeables to be pawed over? And what does he care? Is he trying to convince me to surrender myself to medical science? Then why he would do it all seditious-surreptitious? In one way, he's right. In trading tastures for free speech, I'm selling a kidney to get a liver transplant.

'Time to be quick and choose,' says Wordini.

'I've taken the recommended dosage of research. I've swallowed all your pills. There can be no deficiencies.' The verbocharge has worn off and all that is left is the relentless product-plug of Multipill LipService.

'Is she having an allergic reaction to our offers?' asks Dr Bromide.

'Oh ho, she's a copyrioter. But she'll be back – with fewer options. You'll see,' smirks Wordini and walks out.

I'm not waiting for Dr Bromide to think of a way to keep me here. I snatch up my things and rush out, singing the Multipill greeting as casually as I can, 'Fuel your cells and say goodbye to run-down batteries.'

9

'It was a boobie trap, sweetheart, and we both fell into it bosoms first.'

'Don't try to soft-soap me Mother. You've never showed the slightest static cling.'

The ridiculousness of the Mollycuddle fabric softener LipService knocks the wind out of my self-righteousness. But I won't stop. Even if my anger slips in the silly suds, I won't let Mother blow bubbles in my face. She will tell me why she never did anything to make me feel less alone, to help me understand the tastures.

'I have my figure flaws but I always encouraged you to keep abreast with padded corporate support for a deeper identity cleavage. But you insisted on a natural silhouette.'

'And I suppose now that you've been through the brand's many launderings, you're stainless.'

'I've tried to show you how to use fashion tape so you don't expose yourself.'

'I don't want my creases ironed out!'

It's as if a horrid man in a trench coat has just flashed her. I look away from her distaste but she quickly wipes her face of expression.

'Oh but you do,' You interrupt in house-proud tones, 'you want clothes that are meadow-fresh wearable hugs.'

It seems that You have become more insistently loud-mouthed lately, and it's harder to hear myself think. Sometimes I stray into your goods diction and find my thoughts boxed up in product puffery for ease of delivery. I have to unlearn the limp of LipService. I wonder whether Mother has her version of You – the materialist voice of more – whose bedroom purr promises life as a lingerie shoot. Or perhaps she has believed for a long time that You are her.

Her voice is tired as she says, 'At the time it was part of the sensual hanky-panky of Frisson Froufrou that sold me on the brand, but it's a dreadful body-con.'

For a moment, she actually feels like my mother rather than an exotic dancer who burst out of a giant cake sent to the wrong address and then stayed. She chose FF because she could gorge on satin and silk, lace and ribbons. That could be me. Maybe Mother *was* like me. The difference is just time – time spent with You. Are You slowly forcing me into the servant's quarters with responsibility for little more than manual labour, the moving of limbs?

The memory of the Demoiselles de FF dressing-up game comes back to me through a Vaseline-smeared lens. Yes, it was an exercise in building brand affiliation, but it was also a gluttony of sesame, alfalfa and walnuts that she wanted to share with me. I feel my fabric soften towards Mother, as You say with no hint of irony, 'Home is tender-loving wear – washed with Mollycuddle.'

'The doctor says the corporate wringing and scrubbing has worn away your sensitivity. Will you show me the food stains you still hand treat?' I ask.

I thought she would refuse, make it clear that she rejects the 'body-con' of tastures completely.

She stands very still for a while before saying, 'I'm only revealing this wardrobe malfunction once.'

I wonder whether the revolt of Frisson Froufrou You feels to Mother like a digit desperately scrabbling in the throat for the gag reflex. I think about telling her that the copywriter and doctor were finger-licking over my tastures so she knows she doesn't have to try and purge them. What's good enough for the omnipatchpotents, Mother will surely admit is good enough for her. But then I would also have to tell her how I turned up my nose at their frozen carrots and potato sticks.

Working quickly, she collects a couple of items from the laundry basket and lays them on the kitchen counter. Then she begins to collect items from the fridge and pantry and place them next to the different textiles. But instead of sesame suggestively encircled by a satin camisole, she has a jar of quince jelly, and the alfalfa sprouts that should be married to the chiffon negligée have been cuckolded by a sweet lap cheong sausage.

'But Mother, these aren't the fresh aromas that impregnate fabric fibres.'

'Don't you think I could find a pair of edible underwear blindfolded?' She gathers up the laundry and drops it back in the basket.

Stupid, stupid to question her tastures. It's just that I'm surprised – I thought this would at last be something on which we are in perfect agreement, like satin and sesame. Trying to think of a way to get her to drop her brandface again, I stare at the packet of bulgar wheat, the dandelion greens and tamarind pulp – the strange pantry fellows of the quince jelly and lap cheong sausage. Mother is always looking for new flavours.

Even when I was young, a chef prepared dinner in our kitchen three nights a week. On his off nights, Mother insisted the family dine out at experimental restaurants and roll kohlrabi, dukkah, hyssop and blachan introspectively around the drums of our mouths. Conversation was kept to a minimum. And all of this was made possible by Mother's income and affiliation to Frisson Froufrou. She may not have done it intentionally but she trained my palate. I hadn't thought about it before but without her, I probably wouldn't be able to lickname my tastures. I owed her that as well.

'Is your shrinking experience a relief?'

'We aren't all proud of our kinky tastes, dear.'

She won't admit it, even to herself, but I bet the tasteless world seems like a nightclub visited by day – where all the intensity is lost, and everything feels drained and tacky.

You avert your eyes at any sign of my touch-taste hook-ups – they aren't standardised applications compatible with everyone's operating system. Even if a doctor and a copywriter think tastures are great R&D material, it doesn't mean that they've entered your coding – the commonsumer consciousness. Besides, Wordini and Bromide don't even agree on what my tastures are good for.

Doctors and copywriters are different parts of the same machinery; their sprockets, blades and gears spin at different rates. The danger is in trying to reach between them. Expect to be mangled.

Now that my own fear is no longer a plastic bag over my head, the condensation from my failing breath blurring my perspective, I understand Dr Bromide's sudden exit on Wordini's arrival. Those separate sets of wheels and belts need to be kept a crankshaft's distance apart. If something flies loose at the copywriting end and lodges in the medical mechanism, the whole engine could seize. I enjoy thinking about that for a while.

After spending years trying to hide the tastures that are like a sixth finger, there's no point any more. Maybe it's time to find out what they can really do. I've been thinking about Mother saying she could taste out something 'blindfolded'. Isn't that what Dr Bromide and Wordini got me to do with their desk cubicle? My taste-touch hook-ups mean that my neural pathways are already unorthodox, so what if I could use those connections to start reorganising more of my brain? It would be my own experiment in neuroplasticity. Perhaps I could palpate my way to misdirecting the doctors' wiretaps. By exercising my tactile dexterity, I imagine I might also be able to press my fingers around your throat and make You choke on tastures. And there's the hope too faint to be heard – of words.

I start with what I know and what will earn your approving nod. Otherwise, You'll upset the shopping cart, scattering my thoughts in a violent tamper tantrum. Brand awareness lessons ensure every budding consumer knows the science behind the marketing hook 'more people prefer the taste of our product' – the blind taste test. Only, what is there that's unbranded? The best I can do is tap water, filtered tap water and a bottled spring water – Wholly Water. I plan everything with scientific rigour. All three are refrigerated in the branded containers and marked at their base with a small round numbered sticker. I keep shifting them around in the fridge to help me forget which was which. I don't know if it's You or me, but one of us is trying to keep track, so it takes over a week. You are determined that the Wholly Water – the only commercial brand – be the preferred choice. Preference isn't the point for me, only my ability to discriminate. Which of us is the con artist and which the mark in this shell game?

Seated in front of the bottles, I put on gloves so the aspic tang of the PET bottles doesn't leach into the water. I sense your head bobbing at my shoulder, a fly in my glass. The first gulp settles cool and slightly chalky in the well of my mouth. Must be the filtered tap. In between splashes of water I eat slices of green apple as a palate cleanser. The next bottle slops droplets that I imagine stood pooled in a granite font.

You scoff, 'Granite? Just say what you mean: Wholly Water – rich in trace elements because health is mineral wealth.'

That means the last one should be the unfiltered tap water. There is almost no taste, and its absence is like becoming aware of my own breathing in deep quiet. I check the bottoms of the bottles. I have all three right.

A week later, I repeat the experiment, this time with two more bottled water brands. Your allegiance is now to CellSpring, the market leader. More brands, more bang for You, I reason, but You're getting finger-drummingly impatient with my interest in taste. 'Didn't you learn anything in brand awareness? The classic Popsy versus Folk cola wars? Who cares that most prefer the taste of Popsy if they still go out and buy Folk? Consumers buy brands, not products. Preference in flavour isn't the same as buying intention.'

I start the tasting but I'm muddling through murky waters. Mother stopped by earlier and the air is still hammam-humid with her new floral fragrance, Witchery. The contents of all the test bottles seem to have been funnelled through the perfume's moonflower trumpets. The harder I try to push my tongue past the perfume slick on the surface, the more the water osmoses into tastures – the throat-snagging cheese of the synthetic carpet under my bare feet, the camel's milk of my polyester T-shirt. They seem more real, more present than the water. I only get one out of the five and go around in a fury, throwing open all three windows in my flat.

As I do, You say in your scold-you-so voice, 'I tell you, Popsy and Folk,' before quoting from the research: 'Most consumers can't tell one similar product from another in a blind taste test. But their confidence in their powers to loyally dis-in-criminate between brands increases, the smaller the actual discrepancies in the products' chemical formulations. Drinking cola is a psychological brand experience not an objective one. And you think your little water game is different? Municipal water is still a brand.'

I got it right the first time. I just have to control the conditions better.

A final attempt. It's late and I think I'm getting flu. My throat is a dank highway underpass beneath the increasing congestion. I manage three out of five but at least one was a lucky guess. That's it. I'm done. No more putting things into my mouth – I have other ways of taste testing. Taste is a fly-by-bite sense – as volatile as the chemicals that produce it. No wonder the marketers rely on sensory subterfuge if half their test cohort is likely to be wearing too much cologne or has spent the last hour chewing mega-minty gum. In my gingerbread house of tastures, it doesn't matter whether my nose is blocked or my tongue burned, the walls are always spicy-sweet. Sometimes an urgent texture is a fist pungenting through the horizon of food tastes. Like cat fur – it's artichoke but there are no artichokes like it.

You've reminded me that sight is the sense that sells, the subliminal marketing sense. It's the optic nerve pulsing to the colourful packaging that insists two barely distinguishable cola drinks taste either like Popsy or Folk. Seeing is believing. Tasting or touching, not so much. That's why tummy tamers, booty lifters and thigh slimmers fly out of stores: sleek looks are more real than the crushing reality of squeezed flesh and compressed organs.

'If you ever listened, this wouldn't be such a surprise. Beverages with an identical sucrose content but more red dye are considered to taste sweeter. There's even research into packaging colours perceived to enhance the coldness of beers ...'

Before You can get further into your profit-or-off-it speech, I make sure that You come unstuck. I've had enough of You. For now anyway. The patch thuds dully into the bin. I also shed my shoddings, stepping out on insect tarsi to taste with my toes like a fly. With one foot slaking the hot stuffiness of shoes and socks on the bitter tea of a melamine drawer, the other masticating the carpet cheese, I tie a blindfold around my eyes and reach for the porky savour of the doorframe. Because I'm unable to see, the flavours of things must create depth in the dimensions of sweet, salty, sour, bitter and umami. I imagine I'm in a wire fu harness, poised with the tastes as cables anchoring me to the material world. Pushing off from the lip of the drawer, I arc through the air like a slow-mo stream of Ceylon from the spout of a teapot. I slam into my bed, catching my shin on the frame.

For a few moments, I just lie face down, clutching my leg. The blindfold stays on. When I get up, I move more slowly in my sightlessness, allowing finger and foot to act as a forked snake tongue flicking at surfaces and objects, conversing with the lunchbox architecture of my bedsit.

What I need next is terrain for a new *à la carte*-ography. I visit the hospital park on my day off and walk barefoot. Standing like a pipette, my soles draw up yeasty beer from the lawn, but the grass monoculture is so far-reaching there are no new tastes to mark my progress. I lose track of where I am in the woozy beeriness. Staggering blindly across the vast lawns, I bump into one of the metal signboards in front of a branded flowerbed. It catches my shin just where it was healing from my run-in with the bed. Opening my eyes, I see the plastic blooms of antihistamine pusher daisies with their yellow pill centre surrounded by petals shaped like sniffle-free, peachy noses. The park is too big; I needed a smaller space.

Now, whenever I can do without You, without your words – on weekends and days off – I chew through the designer furniture stores with their wood veneers, Perspex, steel and microsuede. The stock and display mazes are always changing. The routine is: Survey shop floor from the door. Close eyes and part finger lips. A steady pace is important for digestion. Rushing risks collisions with other shoppers. It also doesn't fit with the dark glasses and telescoping white cane taken from one of the Lost Property boxes, which keep the shop assistants at bay. Green matcha, rye and camel's milk help me stay within the lines of the shop-floor sketch as seen from the door and not walk into things. A titbit of cockle is just a corner of the molluscular leather couch. I let the papaya of the cork dining room chairs melt into me. But it's a little side table with a floral pattern of bone inlaid in resin that I can't let go of. Fingers hiccough over the slight irregularities in the table's surface, so that avocado slips into fresh coriander as I try to devour it too quickly. I want to buy the side table but it costs three month's wages. If I could come home and press my cheek into those buttery oils and herbed astringency, it wouldn't matter if I was actually eating baked beans from tins. I want it, want it. I need it, until I realise it needs me.

Like all things, it needs me to polish it and dust it, to walk carefully around it, to insure it, to worry when a visitor places a coffee cup on it, to feel ashamed of making it stand on that dreadful carpet and of having brought it into circumstances unbefitting its magnificence. One thing will probably lead to another – another object of desire. Together they'll conspire for more nights of baked beans. Soon I'll be twisting and tripping through a harem of recumbent chattels. I feel the weight of all these things and my duty to them, and I don't even own them yet.

I remember when I was very young and Mother came home with a crystal-encrusted Frisson Froufrou bra that cost most of her salary. Dad was furious. Now it's me that has You on my tongue and stores in my eyes – even when they're closed. Am I mutating into Mother? Despite temporarily cutting the vocal cords that bind us, your influence is like mould spores – I inhale it everywhere, constantly. Do I have to give up breathing to be rid of You?

10

The gesture of hand to mouth doubles as a sign of mute shame. But that's not the way she's doing it. No, this is the first half of a movement to blow a kiss. I'm fascinated by this abstract expression of defiance. The hand drops back down; the girl on the other side of the Lost Property window is staring at me. I know her. She's Poppy who smelt of condensed milk and bought the first word I sold at school. What happened at her coming of haemorrh-age? Was she one of those whose CVA was a vex-sanguination – a prognosis so feared that everyone genuinely celebrates a comparatively small puddle of blood on the brain?

From my class, Brunfrid and Thea vex-sanguinated and couldn't be patched. No one saw them again. I think of them sometimes when I can't avoid skirting the vexation ward at the hospital with its barred windows and laments from the lifers. But I don't remember it being murmured about Poppy that she had vexed. Perhaps she ruptured while I was in recovery. I still think I would've heard.

Poppy gazes at me the way someone looks at old childhood photos of herself – the recognition is purely intellectual; it barely keeps at bay the sense of estrangement from the figure pictured there. She's wearing the weirdest clothes made of patches sewn together. Pieces of fabric – one with half a logo, another with the printed chicken feet of some brand mascot and a third a dignified floral – have all been tacked together by hand. Wait. I've seen this before, folded in the bottom of an unnamed box that came in yesterday. I've hardly gotten to know it. Running a hand over the patchwork, I chased a variety of tastes, skewering them on the tines of my fingers for a single multi-flavoured mouthful. There was nothing else in the carton except the string of chimes, a few mothballs, a bag of lentils and some loose change. It was one of the emptiest I've ever seen.

Your distaste was obvious when You said, 'Anyone with so few possessions can't be possessed of much consumer sense.'

But now, seeing Poppy similarly dressed in front of us sends You into foaming convulsions of rage. By just standing there Poppy has a more neurotoxic effect on You than any of my grimace-demeanours have ever achieved. I know why. Recycling old clothes refutes the need for the new and dismembers corporate identities. It's brand assassination. On Poppy's top, the Midas Trust bank logo has been decapitated so that only 'das Trust' remains and some sloppy darning makes the 'a' look more like an 'i'. I notice the first starbursts of a migraine and try to focus on Poppy's face.

I greet her in my light bulb LipService: 'Live on the bright side with GlowWorm.' She nods and slides the paperwork for the carton's release beneath the window. My rubber stamp thumps at the forms but my mind is pounding away at other things. I scan for the vex symptoms that parents threaten disobrandient children with – paralysis, facial droop, spasticity, emotional incontinence, dementia ... Nothing. Maybe I just haven't spent enough time with her. The only way to delay her now is to invite her into Lost Property instead of pushing the box through the flap in the wall next to the window. No visitors are permitted in the storeroom but I welcome her in with 'Come into the light'. Once I've opened the door and Poppy is inside, I realise that this hasn't solved anything. What can I possibly say to her and what answers can I expect? She's mute and I'm a babbling LipServant. 'Illuminate for me what's happened to you,' I try desperately. My head is a hotel room that You're trashing. Poppy smiles and takes the carton out of my hands and replaces it with a patch of fabric. By the time I manage to squint through the migraine aura to decipher the words formed by an awkwardly childish running stitch, she's gone. It's an address in the industrial district.

Two days later, I stand across the road from a factory at the address and read its peeling sign, 'Trimcote & Son, Magnetic Tape Manufacturers'. It looks derelict – which feels about right for the place where I hope to amputate You, even if it means sawing off language at the same time. When I reach the iron gate at the entrance, I notice a few kids dressed in patchwork clothes playing in the rubble and ask them to 'turn the spotlight on Poppy for me'. There is some sniggering but they show me a hole in a section of fence hidden from view of the road. The kids lead me down the side of the factory.

In between calls of 'this way, this way', they repeat 'turn the spotlight on Poppy' to each other and titter behind their urchins' hands. I don't understand what's so funny about GlowWorm LipService. I keep my eyes on the ground in front of me, mainly to avoid your poutcry. The kids guide me to a couple of teens not yet come of haemorrh-age and whisper to them.

A girl steps forward. With one hand, she takes the patch with the address from me, while with the other she reaches onto my back to doodle circles with her fingers. The contact jolts through me. No one greets with touch. Brands make first impressions.

She says, 'I am Oona. I will show you. Then you can decide.'

I have no idea what I'm supposed to decide but I nod. If it weren't for the pain in my head, I'd think this was too easy. Are they really just going to let me walk into their tongue-chide community without testing my intentions?

Though I'm keeping my head down, You are upping the voltage, increasing the charge. 'Uggh, her sentences are blander than no-name packaging. No promo-emotional flourish. What do you want with these people?'

I want to fade You out before You and your jingo-lingo become my permanent mood lighting. If they have a way, I have to find out about it.

Oona takes me across the main production hall that no longer has a roof. The window frames have been torn from the walls to construct low greenhouses where vegetables live sheltered lives. A man is stroking and caressing the leaves of a cabbage, as if it's a small rabbit. In what must've been an upstairs office overlooking the factory floor, three women and a man are sorting through piles of old clothes, cutting them up and stitching the pieces back together again. I'm afraid of triggering the fit-inducing GlowWorm strobe with all this brand mutilation but don't know where to look.

I rest a hand over my eyes as if staring into floodlights. One of the patch-makers is Poppy.

She comes up to me and rests both hands on my shoulders, holding me at arm's length and smiling.

'This is the greeting without words,' says Oona. 'Here only the unbled speak.'

Is she telling me that they're all vexed? How many of them are there?

'Is everyone here a blown light bulb?' I ask. Oona looks confused.

'Vex-sanguinated,' I try. But she still doesn't seem to understand me.

'Dull-spoken fools in motley,' You jibe. But I remember reading, at the repository, that only the fool has a licence to transgress.

Poppy performs a pantomime, making the right side of her face droop.

'Oh,' says Oona. 'No, there are only a few true silents. The rest choose not to wear the talking labels. You must choose, too. Then you can stay.'

Poppy takes my hand from my eyes and moves it to my mouth in the stifling gesture she had made at Lost Property. The soft mounds of her fingertips taste of button mushrooms. The other women and man working with her come up to me and brush their hands over my back and shoulders. I'm surprised at the earthy comfort of it, like a bowl of mushroom soup warming beneath the skin.

As we leave the patch-makers, I ask Oona, 'How does anyone know they're on the same wavelength?'

Again my LipService baffles her. 'You mean how do the silents talk?'

'Yes.'

'They read faces. They touch. Our lives are simple. It's harder to lie with the face and fingers.'

She wants me to understand as they do, without words. So I try, but your jab-jabbering is incessant and it's becoming impossible to hold back the pain in my head. We cross a courtyard scullery where an industrial mixing drum has become a hand-spun washing machine, and patchy clothes flap on a line in the breeze like a series of slaps in my face. At the back of the courtyard is a staircase down into the factory's underground car park, where the kitchens and storerooms are. Bunk beds line one wall close to a large wood fire where pots hang over the flames.

'Candle power, literally,' You sneer.

Here, the kettles are vocal and knives chatter on the chopping board, so the people's silence is not as obvious as among the gardeners, who walk as soundlessly as their tomatoes grow.

Occasionally Oona stops and says to someone, 'This is Frith. Poppy welcomes her.'

Then there are more shoulder greetings and back scratchings. I don't know whether these are leading lights or just the people Oona is closest to. I'm still waiting to be vetted, to prove my brand aversion in some sort of anti-corporate loyalty test.

One of the outbuildings is being used as a classroom. An unbled teen instructs the younger children seated at broken pieces of concrete resting on bricks. In a corner facing the students, a middle-aged woman sits observing the lesson.

For the first time, as we stand at the window looking in, Oona offers something like an explanation, 'It isn't like out there, I know. We don't need a lot of words. We only have them for a short time.'

I notice a small boy at the back of the class perform a series of grotesque grimaces and rude bottom waggling. The woman gets up from her chair, grabs the boy by the arm and drags him out of the classroom.

'Some of the children don't like learning words,' Oona says, blushing.

You are spitting watts in an incandescent rage. 'Get me away from these people. They've all been left on dim!'

It takes me a moment to escape your glare and focus on my question. 'What surge protection do you have for when you start to flicker?'

'I'm sorry. I grew up here. I know the words but not your meaning.'

'Bleed ... hospital.' I stumble over the words in the LipService blackout.

'Yes, we go to the hospital when we bleed. They won't help us after that.'

I'm surprised she continues after a pause. 'Some take longer to come back from the hospital. I think they try to live with the talking label.'

She reaches toward my patch, which peeks from below my T-shirt sleeve, but quickly withdraws as if afraid of Polly the LipService parrot's sharp beak.

'Almost everyone comes back eventually. We don't know how to live with all those deceiving words,' she says with unmistakable sadness.

Before I can green-light joining these people, I need to know whether medicorporate oversight will look the other giveaway. If free market competition allows the choice of one product over another, then amping things up to a rejection of all brands should be possible. But I've been wrong before – like at school when Poppy and I were selling words. What if this place is just a trick to force me to choose between the doctors and copywriters? I don't want this to give them a reason to plug me back into their circuit boards in the lab.

'You're not seriously thinking of joining these agrarian-contrarians? They're so primitive they don't even have product differentiation. Don't like dinner? Starve. Don't like our savaged clothes? Go naked.' You sound louder than usual, as if outside my head and not just inside. With the migraine pressing on me from all sides, I feel I'm flickering.

Oona's lips are moving but she isn't the one speaking. The top half of her head has disappeared into blackness. I try to reach out my right hand but my arm hangs taut like the cable to a great chandelier. And the pain, it's unthinkable.

I become aware of myself as bar soap gone soggy. You were the puddle I was liquefying in, my extremities turning to mush. But I can't feel You now. That's how I know they must've taken my patch off when I blacked out. Firm fingers press around my eye sockets and mould my jaw line, pushing through the scum to my solid core. The woman from the classroom is working my skin against my bones as I lie on one of the bottom bunk beds in the underground garage. The pressure of her hands helps me recover my solidity.

For the first time, I notice that Oona is seated at the foot of the bunk. I try to sit up but the woman holds me down and her hands continue to circle my eyes, head and neck like a dog not yet satisfied with its bed.

Oona sees my movement and says, 'I was afraid the phoney words had killed you. But Gudrun has the touch. It's more honest than words.'

I'm not sure. It might be easier to lie with language but touch is still manipulation – even if it feels as good as this.

11

Clothes, toiletries, packets of vegetable seed, lentils and my book from Dad. I put it all in a bag and then take it all out again. The order feels wrong or the uncertainty about going to live with the silents is behaving like referred pain. Should I rather put the book at the bottom of the bag or in a separate pocket? I'm not going anywhere without it, but what if they want to take it away from me? The lentils and seeds are gifts anyway; Oona said they would be appreciated. And they can cut up my clothes and share out my toiletries, I don't care. Just not the book. I rest my hands on Eda-Lyn and press my fingers in circles over her skin to reassure her, as the woman Gudrun did to me.

Since joining the mutes, I haven't had You sneak through the cat flap in my head for a week now. That's the longest I've been free of your visitations since I came of haemorrh-age. Now that your crowding presence is gone, my thoughts are skittish and agoraphobic. But the quiet is already padding the walls. I have joined Poppy in patch-making, where the buds of my fingers taste different fabrics. It's also one of the only jobs in the community that has a residual attachment to language. I enjoy subvertising the logos – with a nip and a tuck turning Prince coffee into Price coffee. Most of the clothes come from landfill. I asked Mother about it once, and she said it was to 'preserve brand integrity'. Donating unworn Frisson Froufrou lingerie to charity stores or organisations damages its upscale image, so instead new bras and knickers are defaced and dumped if unsold.

Oona checks in on me at least once a day. She revises what she calls 'hand words' with me. Of course, they aren't words at all; they can't do what words do – fracture the light of meaning through a crystal lattice to reveal its component colours. They are restricted to the dull grind of manual labour – mimic an action, signify an action. There are only about 70 of them and I already know them. Palms together making a pillow for the head means 'sleep, asleep, go to sleep, sleeping', the fingertips of one hand pressed together and held up to the mouth signals 'food, eat, hungry'. They are the high wall around an abstinent life.

For those who must go as far as to speak, a flat hand at the side of the mouth indicates that a teller – one of the unbled – should be called. This starts a game of charades with the kids guessing at the meaning. The success rate isn't good.

Mainly, it's the younger ones, whose haemorrhages are recent, that ask for a teller. The older silents hardly ever use this last retort. Maybe they're tired of the indignity of playing the fool, or maybe they don't have anything they really want to say any more. Is it possible to no longer want to trace out the topography of language? I can't imagine that. As much as I despised LipService, with its *trompe-l'oeil* ceiling of airbrushed angelic aspirations, I feel the flatness of my scratchings in the dirt here.

The thread running through my patch-making day is the possibility of adding to the hand words. I think of it as my gift to the mutes – a word in repayment for the generosity of these people's touch. Like the head of a tick still attached to my skin even after the body has been pulled off, the itch of your mouthparts says that this is no kindness – *I* want more hand words. I don't listen.

When everyone gathers for dinner in the parking garage, announcements are made. A mute will stand and perform a few hand words. The scrape of the tin drum that is my seat against the concrete floor turns a glitter of gazes on to me. I point to myself to indicate 'I'; next comes my new hand word – I rub my left patchwork sleeve between the opposite thumb and forefinger to represent 'feel'. Heads swivel: there are no hand words for sensation or emotion, which is strange for a culture that prizes touch. It's what makes the sign seem so necessary to me. I finish with the left hand over my heart for gratitude, thanks and respect. Gudrun rises and slowly turns her back to me, and to the table, before sitting down again on her metal drum, facing the exit. The true silents clustered around her follow suit. And eventually so does everyone else at the table. Poppy is one of the last to rise. She looks at me as if I were the monkey who won't release the word candies and so can't get its closed fist out of the narrow neck of the jar. She makes one furtive sign, 'school'. Normally, the sign would mean the community's school on the property but I'm sure she means the one we attended, where we created new words. Then she also scold-shoulders me. I'm left standing. She thinks I'm refusing to learn.

Oona comes and leads me out of the parking garage.

'You've been given a warning. No one is allowed to make new hand signs.'

I make a mute point of shrugging and facial confusion. There's no hand sign for 'why' either.

'It's got to do with the talking labels and brands.' She says the last word as if sliding a hand into a dark burrow in the ground. 'And the way they make feelings and wanting go bad. Some things must be shown by our actions not our words.'

I nod. She leaves me sitting watching the cabbages grow obediently in the last of the day's light.

I stick to the hand signs, but knowing that I can't add to them is starting to make me resent them almost as much as the patch. Oona still makes me practise the signs. I think she's worried. Only I can't tell about what. Whether I've accepted that I can't invent new ones? Whether I'm adjusting or have already been too damaged by the 'talking label'?

One day, instead of asking for the next hand word, Oona says, 'Did you know Avery?'

I can't think who she's talking about so give a slow half shake of the head.

'Avery was my best friend. I knew his touch on my back without seeing him. Poppy went to find him when he didn't come back from the hospital. We're not supposed to look for the ones that don't come back. But Avery was like me. He was born here and he told me he was coming back. He promised to bring me sweets. Poppy says he's dead.'

The carton that Poppy collected. That was Avery. For a moment, I feel like a gravedigger who is caught lifting coffin lids. But she can't know. Lost Property can't be explained in mute point, can it?

'In the box that Poppy brought back were sweets. I know they were sweets because the packet said: "Pop mothballs in, and forget the gnawing worries." Poppy won't let us have them. But I want to eat those sweets and remember Avery.'

Oona's words remind me of the cause of death on Avery's box: 'Fatal haemolytic anaemia due to naphthalene/dichlorobenzene poisoning resulting from ingestion of mothballs.' I had thought it was suicide but Avery was poisoned with words.

'What?' says Oona.

It's impossible to share ideas with people here, but they notice the most infinitesimal muscular twitch of emotion. I ape putting something in my mouth and then keel over cartoonishly. The shame of explaining a death with such buffoonery is horrible.

'The sweets killed him?'

I try again, following the eating gesture with a waggling finger to show that mothballs aren't food, but she thinks I'm forbidding her sweets. Only when I pretend to take a bite out of the end of a candle does she understand.

'So why does the packet use those words?'

With effort, I pull my shoulders back from the defeatism of shrugging. I don't know how to explain the metaphorical mid-air twisting of words that land catlike on another level of meaning. I remember how Dad died writing an echo, burnt by the flame of language. Avery died, a clothes moth drawn to the wordless darkness in a dumb fog of naphthalene. Poor Avery in fool's mothley. His end is as nonsensical as Dad's.

Oona reads my face and says, 'You'll find a way to explain it.'

The next day, while I'm cutting and sewing, cutting and sewing, my mind, too, is stuck on a loop until I imagine my hands as Dad's and guess the meaning of my own mute point – the cutting and rebinding of the stories between Eda-Lyn's skin. The book. With the book I can show Oona the shifty character of words.

There's a riddle that Dad and I loved, which is perfect. And

Oona already knows about guessing games – she has to solve the silents' body-twisters all the time. The thing about riddles is that they're like a weather vane – it's not the compass point, which the arrow indicates, but its opposite that is the answer. And this one's easy enough, if you know about books. I can already hear it in my head:

> Musty moth made a meal of words.
> More's the marvel that in the murk,
> While munching worm's mouth does work,
> It robs the writer of his riddle
> And relishes rare rhetoric,
> Yet retires still unrefined in matters politic.

For Dad and me, the solution (bookworm or booklouse) was itself a metaphor that hatches out of the original riddle as a LipService larva and eats all the books and everyone's speech, only leaving us droppings. For all the words it has consumed and all the words it makes us spout – because more is never enough – they're still just the waste of our thoughts. So am I better off now without the worm and entirely without words? Avery has made me uncertain. What if the mutes' silence is a great unlearning? With every generation, more of them will come of haemorrh-age only to eat mothballs and stick their fingers in electric sockets when forced to step out into the consumerist world. Perhaps the doctors and copywriters are counting on that, together with untreated second haemorrhages and disease.

Aside from me, no one but Dad has ever seen the book. By showing it to Oona I risk losing it. I risk everything.

In the evening, we go up onto the roof with a vegetable oil lamp. We sit on the concrete parapet and I take the book out from under my shirt. Once again, I have pressed Eda-Lyn's skin to my own in a pact sealed in salty squid ink, to protect our hides and the stories concealed beneath them from the doctors and word-eating copywriters. Now I am extending that protection to Oona.

'What is that?' asks Oona.

She pauses as she skates her fingers over the paper of the open page with insect-like delicacy. Eda-Lyn bends her pages in acknowledgement of such a touch.

'Is it a book?'

I incline my head.

'An unbled boy came here with his mother when I was younger. He was looking for books. I didn't understand most of what he talked about. He didn't come back from the hospital. I don't think he liked it here.'

I point to the riddle and she haltingly reads it out loud. Her face has the expression of someone chasing peas around a plate in polite company – afraid to give up the fork but becoming increasingly convinced it's the wrong shape. She rereads the riddle, whispering the words to herself. Then she feels the page again between thumb and forefinger.

'What is it made of?'

I point to the plume rising from the vent above the underground kitchen.

'Smoke? Fire? Wood? It's made of wood.'

I smile, place a fingernail beneath the words 'moth' and 'worm's mouth', before making the eating sign and pointing back to the smoke.

'Insects eat wood. And books,' she says slowly. 'When they eat the books, they also eat the writing.'

I take a large square of fabric from my pocket and watch as she stitches the riddle onto it.

Three days later, Oona haemorrhages. From the patchworking office, I see someone being pushed in a wheelbarrow. I don't realise then that it's Oona. Later, three unbled teens come for me. Angry, they wave the stitched riddle at me, shouting that Oona isn't yet eighteen. My head-hurting words made her bleed early.

I look at Poppy. She knows the basic science of an aneurysm as well as I do. No one can predict the precise moment when the artery wall will fail. Ruptures before eighteen are not unheard of, and to think that any collection of words can increase the pressure is superstition. This isn't like Dad fighting the transdermal to write his echo. Poppy doesn't look up or meet my eyes; she keeps sewing. Out of the window I see Gudrun approaching across the factory floor with two more kids.

Eda-Lyn is at my back. Since showing the book to Oona, I've been carrying it around with me under my shirt. It's just something I have done without defining whether I'm afraid of a backlash or whether I just want to hold the words close, press them through my skin so that, like tattoo ink, they can't be erased. How do I defend my actions without language? Can I rely on these kids who are prejaundiced against speech to communicate for me any more than You?

I run.

12

'Eternal lame' reads the logo on the patch in my hand. A long thread hangs from where the 'f' in 'Flame' has been darned over but the needle that was attached is lost. I realise that throughout my sprint across the factory floor, my scramble under the fence and out onto the road, I must have held onto the patch that I was working on when the kids came into the office. Earlier, when I arrived at the office and saw the tank top with the logo in the pile of clothes on the floor, I snatched it. After the disappointment with the Eternal Flame transdermal, a retaliatory gouging with a pair of scissors gave me a little flutter. The entrailing thread now dangles like gut at my wrist. But none of these patches ever really mend what's broken.

Oona told me I had to choose, and, without really thinking about it, I did. I chose the LipService patch rather than the mute fabric one. When I consider that You are the price I'll pay for that, I wonder if I made a mistake. Now I have to live with a squatter who destroys the furniture. Before I joined the silents, You were taking over more and more rooms, redecorating my thoughts with a hoarder's accumulation of sales catalogues. I barely recognised the contents of my own head. Somehow I ended up paying You rent. I can't go back to that. I can't hear my thoughts spoken in your product hype. I can't. Before I put a patch on again, I need a strategy, a defensive repositioning. Otherwise I can expect to be repossessed.

Soon, I will have to repatch in, go back to the Lost Property cubbyhole. The leave I took when I decided to join the silents is not quite over. No one will have missed me yet. I did wonder how long it would take anyone to notice that I wasn't coming back. A few days? A week?

These last moments without You feel as if a camera has been turned on me. I'm hyperaware, a horrified observer, unable to act.

Without your endless infomercial patter, I register the hustle of my exhalations, the soft suction pop of an eyeball rubbed in its socket and the swamp noises from my gut. Normally your television drone drowns out the burbling. But the truth is that You can't escape my organic chemistry any more than I can. If I hold my breath, which of us will flake out first? And who will revive first? It's a game of chicken. While You're still scrabbling for air, I'll lay out my letters on the triple word score and speak the things that You block with the clutter of your sloganeering. But before I patch back into LipService, I need to practise expelling You with the air in my lungs and calmly holding on to the emptiness.

   I lie face down in the bath, imagining gelatine in the sweet rose water setting around me into a block of Turkish delight. Pink spongey lungs push against pink jelly as if fighting themselves. Calm, airless calm, I tell myself, but every alveolar sac is a throbbing bee abdomen, part of an angry hive in my chest. My head jerks up and the rush of air into my mouth disperses the swarm. The limb-thrashing desperation is not new. It's what I feel every time I notice my thoughts slipping into yours and your yell and sell. So I keep practising until the bathwater is cold.

Once again there's a patch in my hand but now it's LipService – and a particularly repugnant energy drink brand, Mojo (available in such lurid flavours as Red Rush, Blue Beserker and Orange Octane). It's added motivation to suffocate You. And I'm upping the vigilante. I want my words back. When in the blue-lipped moments of hypoxia the air goes out of your palather, I'll speak in ways that no patch would allow, as only someone with unbranded LipService could. My plan is to go to the repository and convince them that I'm a copywriter come to consult the books. They'll open the silo airlock because real expression is unventilated, vacuum packed. It's wormhole logic and I laugh madly at it – the books in their airless silo, me in my airless lungs. I'll fold space and patch physics to get to them. In silent silos, I'll expand the elementary particles of language as I read and write, preparing to unleash my big bang on LipService speak.

There is one problem. What if they recognise me at the reception as my father's daughter? Copywriters are almost always from brand-loyal families with a corporate bloodline. But the proof of unbranded LipService must be in free speech, right? If I can use the magic formulas, they must let me in.

First there's the shock of your re-entry into my atmosphere as the patch takes effect. Being in brand blackout with the silents for so long makes You punching your way back into my head feel like sharp metal forcing through a piercing that's closed over. You come on caffeine-convulsive, giving me the jitters so badly that my reflection in the window appears to be performing a mash-up of moves like someone in the Mojo go-go break-dance battle ads. Your voice has the high-pitched synthetic quality of a recording played too fast: 'B vitaminised! Go from shamblingly shambolic to the metamorphically metabolic in one chug. Feeling flaccid? You're probably low on amino acids. Power up with B vitamins and natural stimulants. Get your Mojo back and go-go.'

I hold my breath until I feel the pressure of the carbon dioxide build up like a shaken fizzy drink. It could just be that the flapping canary in my lungs distracts me, but I no longer notice You announcing yourself. I smugly part my lips and allow air down the shaft. Time to go to work.

No one comes to the Lost Property window. I need to know if I really can short-circuit your brand-cramming verbal programming, so I go to the staff canteen in search of idle chitchat. This is awkward. I hardly ever talk to anyone in the canteen. I don't have friends at the hospital; I just sit and eavesdrop on others' conversations. Who can I call a friend when we are like two radio stations broadcasting on the same frequency, our crosstalk at cross-purposes? I end up sitting alone, hoping someone will appear. An hour later, I leave. I try again the next day and this time someone actually comes up to me. It's the lab tech who assisted Dr Bromide and Wordini with my post-CVA testing. This isn't who I should allow to hear me testing my ability to thumb my prose at LipService, but he's seen me now.

'Say hello reconditioned cogs for better cognition,' says Stillwell.

This is the supposedly 'friendly physician' EmPath greeting that the medically branded use when they want to sound approachable. As one of the few employees at the hospital not patched into EmPath – or confined to the kitchens, like the catering staff – I've heard the white-coated colleagues mutter 'May the morbidity rate never abate' to each other in corridors.

He notices how I become mummified on hearing the greeting and looks embarrassed. It's generally considered a no-go for medical staff to fraternise with patients or subjects. He has crossed the latex glove divide to speak to me. And he did try to help by offering me a way out of selling myself to either the doctors or copywriters. At least I think he did. Right now, he could just be keeping labs on me for the doctor. Either way it would be better to be smiley.

'B vitaminised,' I say with all the Mojo go-go I can muster.

'The sensory cross-activation is still evident, isn't it?' he asks conspiratorially.

I'm confused for a moment. Wait – tastures, he's talking about tastures. Asking whether I still have them. So, he is just scratching Bromide's snitch itch. Only then I remember how afraid I was that those wires and electrodes had destroyed my tactile flavours. He promised it was only temporary. And it was. I don't know what to make of him.

'I can taste the tri-oomph,' I say hiding behind the brand statement.

'I have devoted a lot of neurological resources to imagining your sutured senses and the resulting percepts,' he says resting a hand on my shoulder before turning to walk away.

The wretched fear had made me forget that during the testing he had also given me those little human touches. Really, he used them a lot, like the silents' communing contact. I watch him push through the canteen swing door and remain staring at the spot where his hand was flat against the painted surface, as if by comparing the imprint there and on my body I can finger him out.

I get my chance to try asphyxiating You later when an old man comes to the Lost Property window. As soon as I see his face,

I know which carton he's come for. His photo was in his dead wife's wallet. She carried bits of him with her like a lot of lucky rabbit's feet – a lock of hair, a photo, an old asthma pump with a prescription label on it.

He talks for a long time. His LipService is a backwards and forwards of vinyl scratching, warping language into brand blather so he can't seem to make his request. I let him talk, using the delay to hold and hold. Jaw clamp, fist clench. Tighten the valves to keep myself sealed against You rushing in with the air. By the time he gives up and just pushes his collection form through to me, I haven't breathed for so long that I almost don't register his action in the giddy spin of disco lights that appear in front of my eyes. It's the moment now. I already have my words lined up, little paratroopers that throw themselves into the oncoming inflailation. I open my mouth.

'Bride in the memory slipstream,' I cough.

The old man starts crying.

I'd thought I was more likely to get unbranded talk past You if I fooled You as I was fooled when I heard the Eternal Flame salesgirl in the coffee shop. I had wanted to say 'bride in the memory daydream'. To tell the old man that I know – as did his wife – that he wouldn't forget her. It's based on the Mojo prompt, 'Ride the energy slipstream.' The last word bombs – a parachute that failed to open – but I think he understood anyway.

The rest of the day, I feel a ginseng-zing and then start planning what to try next: one more test run at the corner shop and then the book repository.

Before I get to the till, I jet-puff myself like a marshmallow before cutting off the airflow. I'm a stoppered bottle as I point to a brand in the LipService catalogue. The cashier rings up the amount and I give her two notes and a handful of change. A couple of the coins slip between her fingers. In surprise, I almost allow my imprisoned carbon dioxide currency to escape. I just manage to keep the hatch battened. The cashier is scrabbling on the floor for the lost money. As she comes up, I go down.

Someone gives me a rude rehydrate, dripping Wholly Water in

my face, and I regain consciousness. A couple of customers and the cashier are standing Mo-jiving over me. They're worried I've had a second stroke, so I quickly say, 'The ener-genie is out of the bottle and I've got my Mojo go-go back.' After that, they quickly lose interest. The cashier returns to the till and the checkout queue reforms. I take the LipService patch that I've just bought and leave.

At home my thoughts are feeling the hip-hop in soda pop – with a performance-boosting, rule-the-roosting energy edge. You've bounced back from having the wind knocked out of You and are on a buzz. I never expected You to come on so strong so soon after I stifled you. Is this a vie for a vie since I started trying to gag you?

'That's because with my Mojo, I go from average to anabolic,' You retort.

I'm considering ripping off the Mojo patch even though there's still a good bit of talk time left in it, just to block your energy kick. Trying to focus on what to do, I find myself mumbling the patch replacement routine, 'Strip, double over, dispatch. Strip, double over, dispatch …' I still hear in it a promise to bump You off – off of me.

'Strip, double over, dispatch. Strip, double up, dispatch …'

I pause for a moment over the proposition in the slip of a preposition: 'Double *up*.' What if in doubling You with a second patch – a competing brand identity – I could get your split personalities to shadow-box each other into exhaustion? I would be left to commentate. To boost my confidence at infringing the single-patch dictum, I tell myself that the verbocharge Wordini gave me during the testing was also an additional patch, and it worked. I'm feeling all amino avid at the thought. Doubling up has to be better than inducing hypoxia and barely being able to complete a sentence. Especially if I'm going to convince them at the book repository that I'm a copywriter.

The next morning, I take the new patch out of my pocket. 'Premium Insurance. The best policy.' Its staid, risk-averse, worst-case-scenario worrier could hardly be more different from the energy drink brand's youthful, flashy, always game persona. Off comes the patch backing and without a bungee-jumper's moment of consideration, I slap it on. I sit, a huddled seabird, as the rancid tasture oils my feathers, robbing me of my buoyancy and letting the cold seep in.

It occurs to me that loss adjustment is key; I must adjust to my losses … No, that's what occurs to *You*. *I* must take cover … take out cover? 'Cover more ground with the can-do in a can,' says Mojo You, muscling in. With three of us churning up language, it's going to be harder to know whose words I'm thinking. And the first migraine UFOs have come into view, just like when I first visited the silents.

'Just think energy drink.' The words intrude loudly like a billboard I can't not read. Stop, stop, I want to shout. These competing claims on me must be denied; meaning is sliding about like inflight drinks in turbulence.

Concentrate on walking, I think, going down stairs, moving legs up and down. Mojo makes them pump like pogo sticks. On the street, the bus to the book repository pulls up and I get on. Sweat rides the slope of my forehead. A bus ride, just a bus ride, and then I'll be at the repository to tell them … a dread disease rider pays out a percentage of the death benefit in … adrenaline-ramping, danger-spanking thrills. My head hurts. I can't think in straight lines.

Three stops to go. I watch a girl get on the bus. It's me. I'm getting on the bus. I feel as if my arms and legs have come loose and are floating off. But I can't look away. The protruding eyes and their waxy lids, which are cast down as if watching the multitude of freckles nosediving down the length of her face, are all mine. She looks exactly like me, only she doesn't move like me. She moves like Mother and tosses her hair. The blonde highlights are new; I don't have those. What if she's You? You completely free of me?

I almost miss the stop at the book repository because I'm staring fixedly at the back of my own head. The pain in my skull puts me off balance. Once there, I stagger up the stairs towards the silo's entrance. Then I see You again – just ahead of me. How is that possible? You didn't even get off the bus when I did. Somewhere in my head there's a memo saying it's a hallucination, it can't possibly be real. But out of nowhere fear spooks a herd of neurons into a stampede and that message gets lost. I start running to catch up, to get through the doors before You do. All I know is that I have to be the first to speak. When I approach the reception counter, I can't see You, maybe because my vision is blurring.

'I am a copy ...,' I say and then black out.

I wake up in a hospital bed. Wordini is sitting in the chair across from me. The impossibly straight crease ironed down the length of his trousers unsettles me.

'Well, this has been a rapid dissent into disobrandience. It's been quite the cautionary fail. First, throwing in your argot with that dumbed-down lot – you must spill the scene-by-scene on that place. There's been wide corporate interest in behavioural economic data on the primitivist community and life expectancy without medical care. Basically, whether it's a fizzle or a fad worth commercialising. No, no, don't try to speak. You're getting the silent treatment – no LipService – to allow the postictal neuronal state of hyperexcitation and brain chemistry to stabilise. Dr Bromide's words, not mine. He wanted to bring you in after the primitivist indiscregression. The man has no feel for the psychological long game. But, I knew you'd go all desperado. All we had to do was wait and watch.' He pauses and gives a contented little sigh.

'I couldn't have scripted it better myself: a two-patch LipService overdose resulting in a tonic-clonic seizure at the book repository. Those poor book wardens got into a paper flap imagining you had a nasty mutation of librarian's lung, especially after one of them recognised you from when you used to visit your father. Unfortunately, your double-patch dabbling is not only identity fraud but also LipService abuse. The penalty is your decommunissioning – no more branded patches for you – and refusal of medical care. Without language you are virtually unemployable. Your only option would be to sign on as permanent trial subject in the maim of science. Bromide wins quite undeservedly. You see what happens when you challenge our consumptions? Of course, I can offer you an escapade clause – unbranded LipService.'

13

My full set of right fingerprints is scanned for the contract with Wordini. The icy menthol of the device's glass surface is a knitting needle stabbing up a nostril into the brain. Maybe it's just psychosomatic – after all, I'm consenting to having my skull punctured. In order to sign my release forms, Dr Bromide is insisting that I have electrodes implanted for ongoing neurological research. My contribution to science is in lieu of payment of medical costs incurred as a result of deliberate self-harming behaviour. Wordini was prepared to settle all accounts, but Bromide refused, saying that he didn't expect a copywriter to understand moral responsibility but offenders must perform their community service.

We are in Bromide's office and the doctor is toying with the hand that he's unhooked from the model skeleton in the corner of the room. He appears impatient with the signing process and roughly curls and unfurls the phalanges until one breaks off. He pushes the hand aside in annoyance. 'The subject should be prepped for surgery now. This is cutting into my OR booking, and time management is not an elective procedure here.'

'And now, the index finger here, here, here and here,' says the lawyer representing Wordini. No one gives me a chance to read anything I sign. I'm speechless so it's assumed I'm in a state of shell shock. I try to remember what I know and pretend this is just a little quid pro owe – that Bromide gets to saw my head open and I'll be allowed to use the unbranded LipService while at Wordini's offices but not after hours. I still don't know what I'll be doing for him. Or what other forceps finagle Bromide will perform under cover of the surgical drapes. I tell myself that at least the electrodes should just lurk, unlike You. I'm hoping that with unbranded language You'll have no identity – like a product not on any shelves, You'll just disappear from my consciousness. And I'll be able to write myself back into being, shape myself into a story that can look back at me.

My head is shaved for the operation. As the blades chew through my hair, I feel the metal skim my cranium with a saliva of cold ham. Taste has never swilled over my scalp before; my hair protected me. Being bald makes me feel even more naked than the backless theatre gown. On the gurney carrying me to the theatre, my head sinks into pillowy yoghurt that threatens to smother me. Soon the tasting skin will be stripped away, too.

My skull cap slurps off, leaving my shy cerebral folds bared to the surgical lamps.

'Craniotomy completed. Now let's get the homunculus twitching,' says Bromide to the two other masked men.

I know because I have to be conscious to assist with the brain mapping. My lip jumps or I feel a prickling on my cheek as a spot is electrically stimulated, and I have to toggle a switch upwards to indicate the stimulation of movement and downwards for 'somatic sensation'.

A doctor intones 'motor cortex', or 'Brodmann's three'.

There is no pain, just the rheumatic sadness of a dumb creature. But maybe that is also just the probe scraping the furrow that creases the brow.

When they hit a spot that triggers a tasture, Bromide is instantly transformed by a waggadocio reminiscent of Wordini's.

Waving the probe under my nose, he says, 'Still so sure an independent construal of self can be based on a response that I can induce at will?'

To prove his point he prods at my brain with the electrode, cueing tasture like billiard balls into the pockets of my hand and mouth.

'Patients suffer from collective amnesia about the ownership of their bodies. We, the syndicated medical professions, administer antithrombotics to control intracranial haematoma and limit lesion size. We provide the therapeutic measures to correct loss of cortical function in the language centre. We *own* the physical human apparatus – it is merely leased via a client consciousness to the corporates, until on death it reverts to us. As a shareholder in this carcass,' he points at me, 'I am entitled to dispose of its physiological anomalies to the syndicate's advantage.'

He leans in close and I can't turn my head away because it is held in a clamp. 'That pathologically narcissistic copywriter had better hope that the subject is more commercially viable than her neuroscientific value alone. Because once I synthesise gustatory hallucination in conjunction with branded cutaneous stimulation – as well as auditory and visual cross-activations – and offer it in transdermal format, who and what will *you* be then?'

Although it is the first time he hasn't referred to me in the third person as 'the subject', it feels more than ever as if formaldehyde is closing in around me. I have become little more than a specimen in a jar on his desk. Now that the implants record my neural activity, Bromide believes he can reduce my touch-taste hook-ups to reproducible chemistry and electricity.

The implant is inserted and I register the pressure and impact of the staples tacking my scalp back down. My flesh is dead to me. And I think, the monsters are no longer under the bed but under the covers with me.

I've spent most of the week sleeping, not wanting to know, not wanting to think. Earlier today a nurse took out the staples. Now Stillwell arrives to test the telemetry and recording functions of the neural implants. He fits an elastic band holding a small device in position over the implant. My stubbly head itches and I insert a fingernail under the strap to scratch.

'There's no reason you can't have long keratinised filaments again. The wand,' says Stillwell, tapping at the device on the elastic band, 'will still interface with the implant.'

I nod. I haven't spoken since the seizure because no one in the hospital will give me LipService. Not that I've really tried to get a patch. Learning to communicate using the mute point when I was with the silents has made things easier, although the nurses seldom try to understand.

'I'm going to initiate MindSweeper. It shouldn't stimulate any nervous response,' he says.

My body raises and rattles its porcupine suspicions. But I don't feel anything. I watch Stillwell's hands moving on finger stilts over the keys of his computer and remember his touching parley in the canteen. How do I make sense of the tender raiding of what's in my temples?

Stillwell looks up. 'Good. Now, let's test the real-time reading of your sensory cross-activation. But first, I want to uh articulate …' He bends to rummage in his bag. 'Uh I mean to say, I hope we can form an interpersonal bond.'

I'm almost grateful I have no LipService because I honestly have no words. This is Bromide's creature who'll be prying into my dark matter once a week for the foreseeable future, and what, he thinks we should be friends?

Making a second attempt on the bag, he says, 'I realise that I might currently induce a belief-bias effect in you which is why I hope that this altruistic donation of engineered graft tissue will establish an in-situ attachment.'

He's holding out a square of wet whitish film lifted out of a tray of liquid. I keep my hands folded in my lap.

'It's produced in the burns unit lab from shark cartilage and bovine collagen as a scaffold for regrowing blood vessels and the dermal layer. It isn't supposed to leave the premises due to the risk of industrial espionage, but I thought it would be an interesting stimulus for testing tactile-difference thresholds.'

I place the artificial skin in the spoon of my palm and sup on the woodsy savour of huitlacoche. As the membrane clings to me with its sweaty film, it acts like a suction cup, pulling at memories of dermal contact – the book that Dad gave me bound in Eda-Lyn's hide, Stillwell's touch. I want to like him but the cord from the device strapped to my head dribbles down my neck in a reminder that his gift has the effect of a cattle prod on my neurons – producing just the data Bromide wants. I hand the skin back. He looks hurt but returns it to its tray and slides the container into the drawer next to my bed.

'Tomorrow, you'll be discharged. The day after, you must report to the copywriter. I will schedule weekly times with him to clear your cache and perform data mining. Perhaps we can engage in dialogue then.'

Wordini's offices are in a loft, with unfiltered light coming from clerestory windows above the fixed screens facing out over the streets. The entire floor is crisscrossed with runners for frosted sliding screens that can be arranged to create cubicles or partially enclosed meeting areas. Logos and brand imagery are projected onto some of these walls.

As I sit waiting for Wordini, it occurs to me that, for all this place's self-conscious aesthetics, I've exchanged being boxed into Lost Property for another coop without a view. Why does it matter, when I'm getting unbranded LipService? I don't know but I feel my centre sag like a flopped cake.

A woman appears with a silver tray. She looks at my clothes and shorn head and walks straight out again. She returns a few minutes later with the resentful expression of a child made to apologise, clatters the tray down on the table and leaves in silence. On the tray is a patch. Its transparency is uninterrupted by logos or taglines. Only along the edge is small print: 'Use without accreditation by the Copywriters' Association is liable to be prosecuted as a criminal offence.' Also on the tray is an identity card in my name endorsed by the Copywriters' Association. Next to LipService Pro status, it says, 'For professional use under supervision only'.

For the first time since the surgery, I'm not thinking about the eyes in the back of my head or Dr Bromide giving me notice of eviction from my own body. There's the ticklish excitement of a hamster up my sleeve. Its cheeks are stuffed with hoarded words.

I peel off the patch's backing and smack it onto my upper arm. Out of habit, I find myself holding my breath against You and the rancid grease that clings to palate and arm. But although it's oily, the awful putty note is gone. You are gone. I take a moment and then start whispering to myself – things unspoken for years, such as the word 'dwell' from Dad's echo of Ovid. It's a word with a soft dell at its centre that I sink into like a beanbag chair. And 'relishes rare rhetoric' from the riddle I gave Oona to read. And 'tasture'.

'So that's what you call it.' I look up to see that Wordini is standing over me. 'Not a bad lexicallure. We might hook them with that.' Please, no, he can't take my pet word and let it be teased into endless yapping. He notices my expression and says with a surprising lack of enthusiasm, 'You're now in the world of the lingua banker. If your coinage is not out there earning interest, you risk losing currency and ultimately your rights to unbranded LipService. It's a highly competitive business. Let me show you to your word station.'

Walking between the hazy screens is like flying through cloud; occasionally a break appears in the whiteness and I'm introduced to another junior copywriter. They all look at me with the same disdain as the tray bearer.

When we reach the cubicle that is intended for me, Wordini says, 'I've transferred an advance on your wages. Use it so you aren't always hung by your threads.'

The copywriter's ebrulliance isn't what it was at our previous meetings. It's as if I'm suddenly noticing the gloss of a too-hot iron on his fabric – the inevitable consequence of that implacable crease in his trousers. Of course, Wordini would never actually wear anything with a shabby sheen. But I see his smoothness differently now, as if he knows what it is to be pressed so that the fibres of his being melt.

So I speak openly: 'Dr Bromide is making a patch that will induce branded tastures. I don't know what I can do here to make that redundant.' I'm caught yack-jawed by my own directness – because I still half expect You to intervene and because the last person I heard talk without any brand bingo was Oona.

'I'm aware of Bromide's activities,' he says with a barely suppressed heartwheel of his former animation. 'Even if the doctor can chemjure forth skingestions, who says anyone's buying? They weren't with unbranded LipService.'

He looks at me, enjoying the impact he's made. 'Given the choice, focus groups preferred a whip-sharp quip to the old ad-lib. They liked being able to twinpoint members of their own social tribe.' He pauses and then continues: 'Anyway, getting people to want what is much like a sixth finger requires psychosell – managing the entire experience cycle by tapping the power of association and memory at all touchpoints. That's what you're going to do – give meaning to taste-tactile pairings.'

I'm resigned to enjoying my work. Despite trying to doghouse the sentiment, it won't sit and stay. Wordini pitched tasturising marketing to The Hayrick, makers of gourmet condiments. They approved the proposal, so my desk has been pantrified with pots of mesquite and stout ale mustard, black cherry and anise jam, radish greens pesto, honeyed chestnut spread and more. Now, I have to find a way to make The Hayrick gourmandisers feed on a fondling that's more than in the mouth – a touch that sets the products apart.

I can't make anyone else experience tastures as I do, but I can create an association between non-food tactility and a flavour. Wordini thinks it's enough of a noveltease to experience strange strokings while eating. And I can write tasting notes, copy that binds taste and touch in the mind.

By fashioning sleeves of leather, woven straw and wool to slip over the handles of spoons and forks, I want to take advantage of that moment when the hand and mouth are connected by the implement so that the taste of The Hayrick's brandied nectarines is Siamese twinned with the stroke of satin. I weigh the spoons' balance and heft, adding a bulb below the bowl that hangs ponderous like honey and feels like a lollipop in the mouth. One spoon has a calabash-shaped ladle with a small opening over its gourd so that sipping from it is flutteringly slurpy; another has nodules along its lip – like studs along an ear. Fashioning the spoons from modelling clay, my fingers pull up slips of peppery watercress. Each spoon raises a megaphone to the lips for sweet, salty, bitter, sour or umami. I have planned that a specific spoon will be packaged with certain products, plus an insert describing tricks of taste and buffet-play.

The problem is that most of The Hayrick's products aren't really the kind tucked into with cutlery. So I've moved on from spoons to facial hair in my attempts to recreate tasture. They're fake beards with elastic ear loops to hold them in place and a notch for the nose to remain uncovered, as well as a large hole for the mouth. I called them beards because, aside from covering the same area as face fuzz, one of the first was made of shearling. Actually, the woolly side is worn in, so that it automatically starts muzzle-nuzzling when the wearer's jaws are in action. The Italian beard is made of lace because for me the walnut openwork is a colander for the flavours of pasta, basil, artichokes and tomato. There's also a delicate chain-mail French beard that hams up nouvelle cuisine and traditional cassoulet. Wordini calls them the feedbags but I think that's unfair.

At the end of each working day, I have to moult language and leave my exoskeleton of words behind in my cubicle. The guard at the building entrance has received instructions to scan me for expression – the transdermal's signature – before allowing me to leave. What he doesn't know about is my authorgraph – the writing on my inner thigh that I add to with each bathroom visit during the day. When I get home I trace the letters onto cling wrap. I trip over their humps and tails, unable to form sensetences. My pen staggers blindly forward until I look back over its path to see meaning reassemble around recognisable words. I insert the film between the pages of my book. Words overlaying words.

In those first few days after starting at Wordini's office, I mainly just write lists of words. I don't want to scrub them off in the shower, though I keep reminding myself that they won't be lost – their imprint is on the sheets in the book. As the weeks go by, the expectation that some meddler will snatch away the unbranded LipService loosens itself from me with every washing-off of marker ink. The lists turn into lines, impressions, tastures. Sometimes I come home with both thighs authorgraphed and words clamber-clamouring up my left arm. Sometimes there's just a single phrase.

Stillwell arrives once a week at the close of business with his case of gear. I assume the doctor has arranged this so that I can be interviewed and my words compared with the chatter relayed by the spyware in my head. But since the session at the hospital when he put the MindSweeper system into operation, we haven't talked much. He looks at me over his laptop. His remarkably long neck bows like the top spike of a Christmas tree under the excessive weight of a ponderous ornament. Is this still about the artificial skin? How can anyone who is so sensitive work in the medical professions? If he isn't interested in spreading dominfear of body scientists into us carcasses, why does he do it?

'Dr Bromide has instructed that I administer a course of intramuscular cyanocobalamin injections. I'll need access to the deltoid,' he says.

I pull my sleeve up over my shoulder and only remember too late that the skin of my arm is covered in my personal correspondence. His hand has already closed around my wrist; there's no point in retracting now. He reads my expressions and I try to read his. Do the wordings on my arm (which are actually the end of what starts on my thighs) make me more knowable than I find him to be?

'Mark me, too,' he says.

'What do you mean?'

'Exercise your hypergraphia on my dermis.'

'If you want to show it to Bromide and Wordini, just take a picture.'

'No.' He's already rolled up his sleeve and slaps the opposite hand down on the bare forearm as if trying to coax a shy vein. 'It's not for them; it's for me.'

'Why do you want it?'

'Because it's idiopathic language – without any known commercial aetiology.'

If he is planning on turning missal-blower, I can't stop him. What difference does it make how he reveals my bootleg and batwing letters? After he's injected me a little too hurriedly, so that he leaves his bluish mark, I go and fetch the whiteboard pen. He lays his right forearm on the desk. Mine rests hand to elbow with his, as I replicate the language mutation.

It looks different on him, as though it could walk off into the world without me. I haven't felt that about anything I've created since Faith and I sold Wardsback. For the first time, I think about the beards – that other unknowable people will take them and make what they want of them.

14

'You have a persecutory belief bias. Perhaps because my self-disclosure has not been entirely reciprocal.'

I look up and stop penning in the day's eloquention, shepherding the words from my limb into Stillwell's limbo. I don't know what he does with the armnotes and I haven't told him that I clingingly wrap mine.

'I think I've found a way to equalise the power differential. I'm giving you psychological leverage.'

He hands me a flash drive. On it, I find a series of classified biopsychosocial reports on my mother. First, there was the gift of the graft, and now he's again offering me his professional skin. Giving these to me is in breach of medical obscurity. Would Bromide have risked career kamikaze in engineering this? I feel the rigged mortis of distrust leave my joints.

Resting my palm on the milkwarm skin of his supplicant arm, I say, 'Thank you.' He leaves the office so that I read alone in my cubicle.

The reports are trip-worded with EmPath LipService but not even that can stop my progress down the dark passages:

> Thematic apperception testing (TAT) revealed narratives appropriately constructed on Frisson Froufrou brand mythology but with a disturbing recurrence of an idée fixe relating to mothering infants. Human chorionic gonadotropin levels indicate gravidity. Since cognitive dissonance is an inevitable consequence of these incompatible identities, further investigation is required. It is suspected that having offspring is a method of perceived control over a stressor.
>
> Behavioural abnormalities recorded during observation in a

locked ward have exposed the patient's concealment of a persistent gustatory reflex hallucination precipitated by tactile stimulus. Sustained psychological pressure with concurrent neuroimaging led to an admission. The reproductive idée fixe is rationalised as a coping mechanism whereby the offspring would act as a vocaliser for the psychopathology. Although this represents a form of autistic thinking within the context of the Frisson Froufrou psych profile, the BMG Textile & Clothing Corporation has scored her highly on the identification index and considers rehabilitation financially viable. The BMG Cognitive & Behavioural Modelling Department has requested the predicted prognosis following a course of therapeutic groupthink.

Mother gave birth to me so that, as a child unconstrained by patch programming, I would give expression to her finger flavours. She conceived me as a LipService patch for tasture. So look, Mother dearest, look at me – aren't I just what you hoped I would be? Indentured to a copywriter and mouthing finger foods. I suppose she only wanted what I want. Except that then she didn't. So where does that leave me? Whenever Mother and I connect it's always a bump to the funny bone.

And Stillwell, is he any better? He gives gifts that undo me like wrapping. It seems a Bromidean kindness to show me the records. The sort bestowed with blackhanded compliments that leave their mark. Yes, I have a 'persecutory belief bias', but that's because I see the doctor's shadow everywhere.

I've learned a little from Wordini about how copywriters work out on the unconscious, pumping levers as if on an elliptical trainer. I don't have anything quite so subliminal in mind but I think I know how to get two birds to both atone. Mother will have that talking cure she once wanted and Stillwell's going to get it for her.

'I can't walk the talk out of here. The guard will read the expression signature and stop me. But you can.'

I watch Stillwell's face through the wrong end of binoculars. He seems far away. Until the lenses suddenly drop and he's close, so close. There's a wicked crinkle at his eye, like the folds I darned to delete a letter and subvertise a logo with the silents.

'OK.'

'You'll do it?' I didn't expect him to accept so readily.

'Yes. What do you want to dose for?'

'It's not for me.' That surprises him. 'Bring the patch to my place after you leave. I don't need to tell you where I live, do I?'

He pauses but doesn't answer the question. 'I was a consultant on the scanner design. The guard will register that I'm carrying uncut LipService and not just EmPath. He'll want to see authorisation from Wordini.'

'I could forge it using his encrypted letterhead, if you can get it off his system for me.'

'Good.'

We sit in silence for a moment mentally recalibrating our attitudes to each other.

I feel like it's my turn to warm the bathwater we're in. 'Instead of copying my authorgraph, why don't I give you something of your own?' He wears a wide-eyed happiness like a daisy behind the ear. I pick up the marker pen from my desk and write: 'The naked taste of your skin on bedtime milk rests sleepily at my fingers.'

Stillwell dropped off the unbranded transdermal last night and I hid it wrapped in plastic inside the cavity of one of a pair of roasted quail. No one came looking for it. Today's Saturday and I'm taking the birds to Mother's for lunch.

I haven't seen her since starting at Wordini's office, when I took the advance he had given me and asked for her help to redress my wrongs with a new wardrobe. She was all atwitter over her daughter in a couture pencil skirt working for a copywriter. As she flapped over the choice of heels, I felt like a shop mannequin with sealed fibreglass lips.

In an e-mail I'd sent from work, I had told her in broad chokes about the LipService abuse, seizure, decommunissioning and being headhunted by Wordini. I knew she could fill in the blanks – tasture and prospecting doctors. She's intimate enough with the system.

But, as usual, she chose to only see the Frisson Froufrou frills and not the debtshop workers with iris-less amphetamine eyes.

She even gifted me with a brand-new congratulatory Frisson Froufrou bra to wear. That's the first time she has given me any of her products since the days of the dressing-up box, and those were cast-offs.

I broke the rules, and as punishment those with say-so have given me the great dream of upward mobility. I'm starting to see their reasoning. A nobody can be a malcontent. But the consumer congregation will never forgive someone who spits out their lifestyle aspirations. So now I've been given the finest brand-y wine.

'These briefs – they're not what I'm used to,' says Mother in her damsel-in-distress voice, except that it's obvious she really is afraid of the unbranded patch.

I mime the ritual of stripping, doubling over and dispatching.

'I have a headache, sweetheart.' She extends the transdermal like a lace handkerchief.

Why does she always have to be in character? I should've known how she'd play it, from her romantically sheer peasant blouse and the rosebud bustier underneath it. In frustration, I tear the Frisson Froufrou patch from between her clavicles. There's an awful gagging noise as if I've wrenched out her voice box, and she backs into the bathroom, locking the door. I sit on the couch and try to arrange and revise the questions written on uncooked fettuccine (The Hayrick's, of course) that I prepared at the office. But my rage at being trapped in the role of bare-chested barbarian in her grope opera makes it hard for me to read.

Mother emerges from the bathroom.

'Well darling, are you happy now you've ripped my bodice?'

Her cheeks are lashed with a tear-jerk of just enough accusatory streaks to require comforting but not to make her eyes look puffy. This riles me so much I forget my thwartification and notice that she has at least applied the unbranded patch. But why is she still speaking Frisson Froufrou? Hasn't she realised that the stays have been loosened and she can say anything? I feed her my first piece of fettuccine anyway: *I know you only had me as a mouthpiece for taste-touch hookups.* I see the *folies* Froufrou drop from her like needles from a Christmas tree, leaving her barked and bare. Without a pause, I hand her the next piece: *I want to know when you changed your mind and why.*

'I thought you understood by now that you can't escape the fish nets.'

I bang my fist on the coffee table, making the fettuccine pieces jump as if in hot water.

'I'm tired of doing the tanga with you over this,' she says. 'Frisson Froufrou is all the intimates that I need.' She picks off the patch like a scab and hands it to me.

The unrepentant lingerie lush. Either she can't or won't swear off the brand speak, and I hate her for it. My free hand sweeps the remaining pasta onto the floor and my heel grinds its gist into nothing. I head for the front door, leaving the roast birds. She deserves them. Let her quail behind the FF feather boa constrictor. I'm washing my mouth of the word 'mother'. I won't talk of or to her. Her taste won't touch me again.

Back in my flat, I don't even want to apply the barely expressed unbranded patch. Instead I rub my entire body in a cyclist's embrocation and let the cauterising capsaicin act as the white noise of tasture.

'Did the unbranded transdermal have a remedial effect?' asks Stillwell at our next meeting. The cables from the wand strapped to my head for the weekly download slap at my face as I shake my head.

'Do you still have it quarantined?'

'Yes.'

'I'd like systemic exposure to the unadulterated transdermal, if … if, of course, you waive claims to it …'

Since I realised that my mum fatale is permanently made up, a figment of plasticised emotions, I hadn't even considered giving the patch to anyone else. But I like the possibilities of this idea.

'What if we emanciprated a second patch? So there's one for me, one for you. Then we can talk.'

He rests a hand on my shoulder and at last I feel it – not just the coupling of two senses but two sensibilities riding tandem. So we smile and smile at each other.

Stillwell has brought the second unbranded patch to my flat. I've let him use the bathroom so he can be alone behind a closed door, watching himself in the mirror shape long-unspoken words like bits of bubblegum. Crouching in the kitchenette, I've taken the one that *she* wore. I've never patched into a transdermal that has divulged someone else before. It's contraindicated. I turn my head away from recalling her spoiled tasture and lick the adhesive onto my upper arm without looking at it. The patch's oily mouthfeel carries a backwash of scanties speech and indelicate terms for delicates. For the first time in many weeks, I'm afraid You have returned with a stinging snap of a bra strap. There's a horrid sound of savaged fabric and then I realise it's me – me wailing.

'Frith, Frith,' says Stillwell. His stilling hands are holding my temples. The Frisson Froufrou predations are over. On twisted rankles, I limp around my head but there's no sign of menace.

'I'm OK.'

We sit back to back on the rug. It's comforting and he's still muddled by hearing his thoughts unrefracted, so it's easier if I'm not looking at him. He starts by trying to explain his gift of artificial skin.

'So it's not just that the dermal template tricks the cells into healing. It tricks them into regeneration rather than scar formation. But it also eventually dissolves. It's a ...' His excitement outruns his shuffling words. 'It's a histological copywriter. It directs the expression of dermal tissue. And that's not all. Did you, did you know? After the graft has taken, pain is the first sensation to return. Then touch. Cold. And finally warmth. Think ... think of what it says about us ... in, in evolutionary terms.'

'Oh, evolution-devilution,' I swipe. 'Pain first? Sounds like a doctor's order of infliction.'

He doesn't respond but his back becomes a hard boulder.

'You aren't like Bromide. Why would you want to be in the medical professions?'

'My parents are in the medical professions,' he says too quickly. He's quiet for a while but fidgets about, playing dodgem cars with my back.

'Actually, they were worried ... about the necessary med-side manner. Because of my disability. I had chronic vocal tic disorder.'

'What's that?'

'It started when I was about eight. With the Snuggle-Ups digital pet slogan. I'd burst out with it. Burst out in a high-pitched voice. I didn't want to. But it came out. Had to come out. Pent-up, pent-up words shook loose. Bit like now.'

For the first time, I consider that giving up EmPath also meant giving up his wordulous fluency.

'In an aneurysm preparedness class, I yelped "Stoked on strokes!" I was almost expelled. Lucky. Just lucky I had been recently diagnosed and that I was in the EmPath community. If my family had been with one of the corporates, it would've been the profane asylum for me. If the tics are coprolalic. That's what happens.'

I feel his body release the ticcing bomb and relax. He speaks more easily.

'The tics quietened down before I came of haemorrh-age. When I ruptured, they disappeared completely. Because they were always taglines or sonic logos, I knew. I knew the ... the oafishness of transdermal language programming long before anyone else my age. And the urge to tic – it's not so different from compulsive consumerism. But no one can hold out against the consumptive tic forever. Everyone capitalates to it in the end. Everyone.'

His back is heavy against mine as if the spine has crumbled. He turns and rolls onto his side on the carpet and I can't tell if his eyes are even open. I'm about to tell him that I haven't capitalated but then remember that I'm still wearing the day's business bedeckings dictated by the season froufrou.

'You shouldn't think medicine was just a default choice,' he continues. 'I spent a lot of time in consulting rooms. In habit reversal training. In biofeedback machines. I know what doctors are like. But look at you. You with your cross-modal interaction.

And look at Mrs Waxwing who has palinopsia. Yesterday she saw a persistent afterimage. The Nice Slice emblem from the hoarding over the restaurant. It's across from the bus stop. For an hour after catching the bus, the pizza sainted anyone she spoke to. "A thin-crust halo", she called it. And there's the fourteen-year-old Holbein boy. His hearing is impaired but he has auditory hallucinations of jingles – especially the symptoms jingle. Sung by an eerie children's choir. These are the human conditions that people my days. You remind me that biology rejects grafted brand identities.'

'It might be the secret brandshake of a professional rather than a consumer tribe, but EmPath still enforces an identity,' I interrupt.

'I know.'

He sits up again and shakes the pins and needles out of an arm.

'But that's what I was saying. About pain. Pain is the first sensation to return for burn victims. You can't be *la femme* Frisson Froufrou or ... Prince coffee royalty or ... a doctor. Not with real pain. Then you can only be yourself. I'm good at what I do. Because I understand that.' His head is lifted on its long neck now and with the light behind the wispy haze of blonde curls, his head is like a thistle on a stalk.

'But you'd be even better if you didn't have to speak EmPath?'

It's a few days since Stillwell and I spoke unbranded LipService. There's been an accident, and the bus I ride to work is taking a different route to its usual one. It turns onto the motorway and passes a large Frisson Froufrou billboard. Leopard crawling over what appears to be bearskin, the underwear model looks out at us with that startled-deer expression. She's partially obscured by an outburst of graffiti: 'Where to hide when your hide is a patch of lies?' It's one of my authorgraphs. The row seated next to the window turns to gape at the sign.

'What brand is that?' asks the woman next to me.

I shrug and bite my cheek to stop myself grinning. How did he get up there to write it? It must've required ropes and harnesses and daring. I wonder if there are more. While I'm tucking my armnotes away, he's been writing them large.

15

It's launch night for The Hayrick pop-up restaurant. I don't know what to expect or even what to hope for. I've had my head stuck in the cloudy glass of my cubicle. In a vague unarticulated way, I suppose I imagined I was creating savoury textures for Stillwell alone. But I'm not. As Wordini said, 'This is the beta phase for the tasture tablewear. If you can serve up the tastemakers on an indoctrinplate, we can cut ourselves a nice share of wallet.' And what if I hit the buyers' spree spot? Do I want that? And what if I don't? Which is worse?

The diners wear blindfolds, my French chain-mail beards and big bibs. A set of my spoons hangs from long cords around their necks so they can't lose them. In the lift down to an abandoned underground station, the attendants put on their thermal imaging goggles. They lead the influencers and opinion feeders to their tables to take up their suppersitions. Above ground in a small recording room, Wordini watches the red-green-blue human heat signatures from the infrared camera. I sit next to him.

Even though I know that the diners can't see them, the stalk-eyed attendants carrying in the entrée work on my nerves like the horrid high-pitched shrilling of a dog whistle. I know I can't say anything to Wordini because this was his pragmatist's solution to serving people food in complete darkness. They're just wrong as part of my tasture opera. But I don't have time to ponder why. Already the spoons with the knobbly lips have skidded off in hot pursuit of mushrooms stuffed with The Hayrick escargot.

'Ah, it's epiphanised eating – a fork-tender, molecular deconstruction of songbird hearts infused in *joie de* garlic butter,' bellows a large celebrity chef. Just because the banquothers can't see each other, they all seem convinced that no one can hear normally either.

'That's a load of meat-factory pink slurry,' shouts back a retail-chain buyer directly opposite him. 'Can't you savourise the *sous-vide* aubergine with a hint of tarragon and longing?'

'And what about these?' says a woman, clinking her beard. Surprisingly, everyone appears to hear the slight tinging perfectly. 'They bring out the full eruptive demeanour of the victuals, *n'est-ce pas?*'

'There's a definite umami about the whole brazen enigma,' agrees the chef.

'I prefer the nipple-grazing lip of this spoon as it rises from the unmade bed of fennel,' says someone else.

In self-congratulation, Wordini slaps my back and gleefully crows, 'They're swallowing it like foie gras geese with the gavage funnel down their throats. No pseudy will ever admit to having lost the pot in a dining experience.'

'You make them sound as oblivious as the character in *CEO Sindy's Selkie Suit*,' I say miserably, although I suspect that this is really more like *The Emperor's New Clothes* and I am the weaver who has spun the invisible robes.

'What a droll little banalogy,' he laughs.

'So are we going to explain tasture to them, the way the textile technologists do for CEO Sindy and the management board at the end of the story?'

'What in mirth for? Then they would have something they could bespittle with their sharp tongues,' he replies.

'If this is what you had in mind all along, what did you need me for?'

'My dear dupe, I could never have come up with a hoodwink as genuinely shamboozling as all this. The spoons, the beards, the darkness – no amount of my weasel words could achieve it.'

I turn back to the screen and the naked heat of the bodies. There are bits of food caught in the beards now, morsels and sauces dripped all over the table linen. Although they've learned to adjust the volume of their voices, they've also quickly adapted to the leeway blindness gives them to scratch itches and fully aerate a mouthful while talking. It's all so very ugly. I look at the carpet between my feet because I can't bear seeing this crookery of tasture, knowing that I scammed it into being.

At the end of the meal, the tastemakers are brought back up to the surface. They spend a few minutes in a dimmed room, removing their blindfolds and bibs and cleaning themselves up as their eyes adjust to the light. Together with The Hayrick execs, Wordini and I wait to receive their impressions over coffee.

Since getting unbranded LipService, I've spoken only to Wordini, some of the staff in his office and Stillwell. With branded patches, no one says the wrong thing – or the right thing. I feel self-conscious and more than self-conscious – afraid to speak.

The opinion feeders start arriving in the reception area. I manage to stay out of the hobmobbing by making my coffee with the slow deliberateness of someone modelling a ship in a bottle. When I can't delay any longer, I turn from the table and am instantly cornered by the celebrity chef. 'So you're the little saucier who cooked up this *amuse touche*?' He taps my forehead with one of my spoons still hanging from the cord around his neck.

'Uh ... yes.'

'You must know,' he says conspiratorially, 'that my *métier* is really the ambrosialisation of harpoon-caught lexicon served drizzled with gastrosexual promise. Half of dining is menu descriptions.' He winks.

He looks at me, anticipating some response, only I have none. So he forages on. 'Of course, with your sensory palate cleansers, flavours sigh to a liquid-smoke climax.'

My gratitude flashes flambé blue. I think he understands something of what I was trying to do. 'Thank you, I'm so glad you feel that way.'

Encouraged, the chef continues. 'So you'll give me a toothsome *soupçon* of your recipe?'

Behind him Wordini is violently gesturing for me to zip it. I'd like to enjoy the irony of the copywriter trying to enact a mute point like a silent, but earlier he'd threatened me: 'If you break the ruse, those will be your infamous last words.'

While I can't tell the chef anything, I want to show him my

appreciation. I rest my hand on his shoulder and am about to say how sorry I am that I can't help, when he recoils under my touch. With a noise like a balloon animal being twisted into shape, he withdraws, disappearing behind a conversing group of The Hayrick executives and retail buyers.

In the shock of the moment, I find myself wondering about Stillwell. Would he have known that some people react like this to touch? Probably. He seems to have a better grip on the LipService mindset than I do. I attempt to scale its glossy heights but like a spider trying to escape a bath, I always slip back.

Wordini is laughing hard. It takes him a while to recover enough to speak. 'Pseudies can't ordeal with uncomplicated sensory input,' he explains. 'It's like serving them plain, unsalted rice. If the grains haven't been cajoled, poached in brand bouillon and given symbolic fluffings, they would rather starve than eat them.' He starts laughing again. 'You didn't actually think being a foodie had anything to do with sensual experience?'

Wordini calls me into his office. 'My trend patrol brings us good sidings from the front lines.' He hands me photographs showing people wearing my beards and spoons as they walk through shopping malls, receive pedicures and draw money from ATMs. The pop-up restaurant closed two weeks ago, and a limited edition of The Hayrick hampers with the spoons and beards is available at selected stores.

'But ... none of them are eating,' I say slowly, trying to train my confused ideas over this trellis of the obvious.

'Yes, isn't it a coo-coup – everyone cooing all cuckoo over your product coup? Now try and say that fast!' he says, guffawing at his own wit.

The beards are starting to take on a life of their own. The trend patrol's pictures show that, while some women continue to wear them as a sort of high-fashion yashmak, others drape them like triangular kerchiefs over their heads. Both sexes attach them to belts as suggestive loincloths over jeans, with the mouth hole rather obscenely positioned at crotch height.

While I'm looking at the pictures, I have to keep reminding myself that I made the beards. They are *my* creation. But I can tell myself that as often as I like, it's not true. A realisation comes like that sense of falling that wakes you with a start. It's as if a LipService of objects is at work. Some monstrous genetic modification occurs as my ideas reseed from me in distant soil. How could something that comes from me sprout strong and alien – true products of the consumerist dirt? I suspect your involvement; I suspect a side effect of the implants. My suspicion roves, it beats at the air but finds no perch to rest on.

After seeing my bespoiled beards, I left a message for Wordini before quitting the office, saying that I wasn't well and wouldn't be coming into work today. I just want to pick up my pieces. But now Wordini is yelling down the phone at me.

'If you want your every boo-hoo pandered to, you should've survendored yourself to Dr Bromide. So unless you're having a rupture, I own your fat farce and you'd better get over here.'

In my unpatched state, all I can do is make a small groan of assent.

When I arrive at the office, it becomes apparent that Wordini's snooper troopers aren't the only ones who've been watching the beards' depurposing into status symbols. A number of corporate clients have contacted Wordini saying they also want what he refers to as 'spoondoggles or some such parapheregalia'. I sit in my cubicle and think about starting all over again, knowing that no one – neither the corporations nor their customers – gives a discount coupon about what tasture really is. I can't bear to watch what I feel being commercially abominmated again. My forehead sinks into the sour rye crust of the desk. The only way is to fake it. It won't matter anyway. I've learnt from the pseudies – everyone just wants a slice of crispy half-bakery.

I develop a pitch for scent diffusers that release blasts of newly mowed grass in a DIY chain. My first choice was freshly sawn wood, but Wordini's research indicates employees were considered 'more fix-it fit' when planted in a meadow of a grassy olfactor. For Nice Slice pizza, I design a scratch and sniff takeaway menu. That's when Wordini comes to me, waving the mock-up and announcing his presence with a zephyr of anchovies and cheese.

'Where are the fingerfoods? I gave you Nice Slice so that you could induce a Pavlovian product response,' he snaps.

'But this triggers salivatory pooling much faster than the drool-down effect of the beards. I've read papers from the database about the olfactory bulb's location within the limbic system and direct access to the amygdala and hippocampus, which makes for more powerfully conditioned associations with mood and memory than other senses.'

He looks at me with narrowed eyes and I'm suddenly so nervous that, without even touching it, I taste the tension in the high thread-count of his suit as a metallic note. The release of pressure is sudden as he turns to leave my cubicle, saying, 'Botch your step and I'll have you scotched.'

The projects keep coming. My elevator concept for the Arcadian Group of hotels adds real vibrandcy to the chain's signature experience. Even Wordini gave cred so. By selecting a floor, guests also engage an ambience. For the suite level, projections on the elevators' walls make patrons feel as if they are travelling between the canopy and floor of a rainforest. Instead of music there are surround effects of dripping water, calling birds and the shrill of the katydid.

I feel the warm hug of smug as I produce these forged experiences. At the launches, unveilings and openings, I've even learned to make appropriately ambogus statements such as, 'Yes, the rainforest ambience enhances a form of psychological levitation, of leaving behind the surly-burly world beyond the hotel doors.' I tell myself I'm fooling everyone, that I can huff and puff and blow them all away. But the workdays just never end and my eyes are soon shackled in black rings. 'It's a form of psychological levitation,' I repeat at product parties. And I'm too heavy to rise to anything else.

Everything – my words, my ideas – seem to come out of a price gun, the same little sticky labels. Today, the sell has run dry. I'm coming up blank on the Skidoo retail concept. I have nothing. Just nothing. They sell ski equipment. I watch the promotional videos. All I can think is that things would be better if I were on skis.

At lunch I go to a Skidoo outlet. I buy skis. I stand on a plastic slope. The gliding is nice but I still don't feel it. Maybe it should be cold. It's the only thing I can come up with. Make the whole store very cold – wintery.

'That's not a sham dunk! It's so bleedious, I'm surprised I haven't haemorrhaged,' Wordini says in disgust. Failure, failure. I've failed even in fakery. I think of Lost Property – a box with my name on it. It's empty. I'm empty and dead. To fill me up, Wordini prescribes a malling – I must 'regain purchase on materialism', he says. He expects certain 'spend-swift ways' of his staff. That means 'presenting proof of investments with an appropriately high cost-to-status ratio' in the form of receipts.

At the shopping arcades, I get comimmersed in dresses and scarves. I drape, swathe and cloak myself in cotton, linen, satin, silk, neoprene and grosgrain. Automatically my mind gets into the weave of catchpraises – *wear the kindest cut of all, putting the neo in preening.* I devour so much yoghurt, ricotta, sesame, cool mint, beeswax and drippings that I feel a bit sick. Still, I must stimulate the wardlobe of my brain. Keep going, I tell myself, clutching at handbags, grand bags, tanned bags – *because life holds more with a designer bag.* I know I'm spinning too fast and am losing words' worth, but if I can't brandstorm, fire off a stun-pun, they'll take away my language. I even go back to Skidoo and buy a downy parka, snow boots and earmuffs. But the hot stuffiness of trying them on stifles any other ideas.

I stand outside the door of the flat with my shopping bags, keys in hand, but I don't want to go in. Since being pro-opted by Wordini, my flat has closed in on me. Gangs of goods wield their sharp edges in the shadowy alleyways between boxes of material indulgence that I've never unpacked. All these things wait for me. They lurk. I lurch. They throw themselves at me. Sharp heels and kicking toes of bitchy stilettos. It's as if they know I'm foundering in their ostentnarration. Reaching for the light switch, I'm pelted by a collection of Fabergé eggs. I beat a retreat to my bed, where

I have to fend off the advances of the greedy guava-walnut-melba ensemble that reclines there. I'm grateful to sleep.

The alarm goes off in the half light. My mind tears loose from my body in shock and my limbs can't find their way home. An arm connects with something hard, and one of the skis falls like a guillotine on my head. The rabble of revolutionary un-a-wares cheers. My head hurts and my vision jumps like the picture on a bad TV screen.

Through the blur, I notice a movement at the front door. From the hood of the Skidoo parka that hangs on the hook there, I see a face emerge. My face. But it's elaborately made up – as if I were Mother. She that's me approaches the bed with an awful painted smile. All my great and goods rattle with excitement. In her hand she holds my spoon – the one with the mouth-filling bulb – and a beard. She moves towards me with swaying hips, the snake in the gross sales. And I know – I know without a doubt she's come to wedge the silver spoon in my mouth and tie it in place with the beard.

'Mild concussion as the result of minor head trauma,' says Stillwell to me in the hospital. Although I've seen him weekly at the office for the MindSweeper downloads, we haven't been able to meet for an unbranded speakeasy for months. 'You've been certified invalid for two weeks – although you'll be discharged tomorrow. You'll need to remain recumbent. I'll increase on-site neural monitoring.' I dip my chin into a nod and feel a stab in my head. Any relief at escaping the office is sold down the shiver by the fact that I'll be deworded for all that time. My stock will be downgraded.

Stillwell arrives to check in on me at home. He looks shocked at how my flat has come under pretsiege by status goods and carefully picks his way through the tortuous terrain of pricey, pretty things. While taking data readings and doing the neural checks, he seems more withdrawn than usual. I miss the little touches. When he's done, I get out the two unbranded patches left over from last time.

'What's, what's all this ... stuff?' he blurts out as soon as he's patched in, waving a hand around the room.

'Investments with an appropriately high cost-to-status ratio,' I say.

'I thought you didn't care about … about things.' It's an accusation.

'Spend-swift is a corporate responsibility of all copywriters.'

'So? You don't have to keep it. Sell it, sell it all,' he says.

I hesitate and his face takes on an expression of disnay – a hardening against me.

'But I need it to get into the products' spin so that I can transprose the buyological urge.'

'They're, they're …' I can see his thoughts engaged in a furious stock count of words. 'They're con*tumour* goods, understand? Con*tumour* goods!'

He starts fiddling with the edge of his patch as if he's going to tear it off and walk away. Instead he looks at me and says, 'You know, you're talking like him.'

'Who?'

'Wordini. You're talking like him – even when you don't have to. The armnotes were never like that. Are you still even making those?'

I haven't written an eloquention for weeks. I've been too busy writing commercenery rhymes. I look at my hands even though hanging my head hurts.

16

The noosey parka is keeping to itself. I stare at it hanging on the door. I squint and look atrance. But it remains unanimated – a legless back turned to me as it hides its face and perhaps a gallows-knot in its sleeve. But she that's me doesn't appear.

The censuring ski has done me a kindness. It's given me time to think about how I got from working on the beards to where I am now – from an empty flat to one beset and bethinged, and from Stillwell's expression when I wrote the armnotes to his face when he saw my advertising hoardings. There must've been a moment when I made a You-turn, chose to peddle indulgence and commodeify my life. Only there wasn't. I didn't surrender to You, and I haven't become mirage-me with the awful painted smile. Have I? All I wanted was unbranded language, but somehow that single desire mutated through rapid sell division into a legion of splurge urges. One desire in life is never enough for the conspicuous consumer. On every street corner, products are out soliciting with a wink and a smile.

Suddenly I see the parka jump and twitch. I'm so afraid of the return of the proxy-mate that it takes a moment for me to connect the jacket's spasms with the banging sound. Someone is beating at the door.

Stillwell comes in. I wasn't expecting to see him; he must've snuck off on his lunch break. He's flustuttering so much that I can hardly understand him. I pull out the unbranded patch from a drawer and offer it to him.

'Can't, can't ... must ration doses based on priority determinants,' he says, waving away the patch. 'Now, now ... I, I need your full stethoscopic auscultation. No attention deflit-um-um-deficits, please.'

I nod with deliberateness, as if the action can slow the syllables' tripping feet.

He takes a breath. 'You see, I consulted with Dr Bromide.'

That name – it's like a glinting in the glass eyes of stuffed animals. I think Stillwell notices but he ploughs on anyway: 'Your recent occupational readings show decreased activity in the right dorsolateral prefrontal cortex and right middle frontal gyrus during presumed phases of reflection, while activity increases in the right posterior cingulate cortex and the right middle frontal gyrus during phases of inferred problem-solving. This presents a classic neurological pattern – clinically unmistakable.'

The EmPath LipService is taking him to the dry cleaners. I imagine him plastic clad, swooshing along the motorised conveyor, hustling along a closed loop of meaning. I know that's ungenerous of me.

He snaps his fingers at me in annoyance. 'You're allocating insufficient neural processing resources to my articulations. This is important.'

I use mute point to indicate that I don't understand.

'Then read for yourself,' he says in exasperation.

On the tablet he hands me is a screenshot of a document. It's the agreement that I signed in Bromide's office. But now I see that I was never one of the contracting parties: only Wordini and the doctor are. I was the subject of the transaction. Stillwell points to a clause headed 'Planned obsolescence'. It's written in the usual legal fata arcana that shimmers on the horizon of apprehension. Wordini is granted the mind rights for exploitation to the point of depletion, at which time the human resource reverts to the original owner, the medical professions syndicate and the management of Dr E Bromide. Depletion is defined according to the Maslach Burnout Inventory, with special reference to the emotional exhaustion and depersonalisation scales. The implanted intracranial EEG readings should correlate with job burnout and validate the stress-dependent disruption of prefrontal function.

Stillwell points to the passage about job burnout. 'That's the neurological pattern I saw emerging from the implant data.'

Talking more to himself than me, he adds, 'He didn't expect that I'd abstract the data to reach that conclusion. Thought he could keep the procedure of contracting out your aversion therapy clinically silent. But I heard the arterial murmurs.' He pauses. 'If it weren't for your minor head trauma, my prognosis is that you would've reached the symptomatic tipping point fairly soon. Dr Bromide's treatment strategy is remarkable … He would have successfully triggered a chronic inflammatory response to language through its association with the detachment, cynicism and impaired empathy of burnout. By using the copywriter to act as an intermediate host to incubate his antigens, he avoids the adverse effects of white coat hypertension. And liability risks.'

I tug at his sleeve to tell him to go slow on the Gorgon-like med-user talk. It takes more sleeve snatching, but eventually I understand. Wordini is supposed to work me to word weariness, nonosyllabic indifference. So that when he returns me to Dr Bromide I'm cured of caring and go meekly to dissection. What grates is Stillwell's admiration for the doctor. So maybe Bromide out-conknifed Wordini? The cut and thrust never touches them. But on a bright day, I can see the lacerations the two of them have left in my shadow. Does it matter which one of them sliced at my throat or who left the silhouette of my fingers hanging by a thread? I despise them both. And I want him to hate them, too.

Stillwell leaves in a hurry but he says he will be back. The door closes behind him. I am alone with my parasitprized possessions, and I'm starting to feel like a tongue caught behind the clenched teeth of my trappings of success. How very LipServiceable that the success is illusory but the trappings aren't.

Before I can properly reason through what the contract means for me, the horror of its implications sends tremors through me, as if a patch jolt were stirring my tectonic states. I have to bite-knuckle through the falling mental plaster to think clearly. I'll be sent back to Bromide and there'll be no more pure LipService. Will he even bother to give me any language at all? It won't be like going to stay with the mutes. There'll be no tell trail to return to. That really rattles loose the quaking. Stillwell would probably tell me this is just part of the concussion. But I don't believe that. I want Mother's suede purse so I can hold on to the taste of seaweed through the heaving, the way I used to when repatching into branded LipService. Scrabbling across the floor on hands and knees, I go searching for it. But I don't know where among the boxes and merchandise it has gotten to. There are too many things. Stillwell was right about that, I have to rid myself of these special effects. I stop looking for the purse, sinking hopelessly into the well-aged rind of the nasty carpet.

It takes a few minutes sunk in the funk of stinky feet before my mind settles like dust on what I really want, what I've always wanted. And I know where to find it. Inside the broom cupboard is a broken robotic vacuum cleaner. I open its bin and take out Eda-Lyn from her hiding place. It has been a long time since I held her. I slide my hand up the leather arch of her spine, and my skin sops up the taste of squid ink. It swirls across my palate and behind my eyes, blotting out the world and all my hoardings. Now if I slip my fingers into her and the forbidden tang of paper, the dark cloud will resolve into sepia lettering in a rush of words over the page. But I wait. I hold back. I wait in the ink well with only the sound of my breathing. The primordial sepia soup fills my mouth, my throat, my lungs. Teeming, teasing within it are single cellular ink blots and a restlessly recombinant DNA alphabet. At last, I slide into the soft chickpea warmth of a page and feel the words released into me. They shout so loudly I almost believe I've spoken them.

I lie on the linoleum of the kitchen floor, although it's more like I'm levitating because I'm unaware of its raw onion flavour. There's only Eda-Lyn's sweaty brininess as I throb to the echo of a silent ejaculation. The 'contumour goods' have shrunk back now; there's more space in the flat. With Eda-Lyn, I have the answers. She is the answer.

'Is that really a, a …?' asks Stillwell.

'Yes, it's a book.' I hold out Eda-Lyn for him to look at.

His hand reaches tentatively, as if uncertain whether the tanned hide is just playing dead.

'I've had it for years. You won't get sick,' I say.

We've both patched into the unbranded transdermals but there's not much talk left in them. It would've been too suspicious if Stillwell tried to smuggle out new ones while I'm off work, so we have to keep it short and of import. There's a lot I have to explain, and I'm afraid I'll end in stutter failure before it's all said. That's why I need Eda-Lyn to speak for herself.

I let him start by reading the frontispiece – the story of how a doctor cured Eda-Lyn after she died in the almshouse, so she could serve as a trophy of his discovery of the pork tapeworm in the human body. He stuffed her full of his EmPath.

The thing is, Stillwell is sEmPathetic. He believes in the medicause. He doesn't just see it as the sticky side of the LipService patch, the equally essential reverse of the logoed face. So I don't know what the words in the book will mean to him. Among the mutes, new words were as much a contagion as books are to the branded. I call up the memory of the subvertised billboard with my armnote on it and try to hold it in my mind's eye, but the thought of how he marvelled at Bromide's skulldiggery pulls me away like the movement of the bus I was on when I saw it. He did come to warn me about the burnout, I tell myself. He did.

Stillwell has finished reading the frontispiece and is rubbing the book's leather binding against his cheek, as intensely absorbed as a twitcher listening for a rare bird's call. He's paged past the horror that I first felt at her mortal remains and gone straight to taking her between the thrum and forefinger of fascination. Is it his laborhetorical thinking or just that he's someone who makes gifts of engineered graft tissue?

'I can't feel the difference,' he says.

'I can.' Eda-Lyn could never be like any other leather. We look at each other. He looks away first and, even though he must know it's a dangerous professligacy, wasting what's left of his patch, he says, 'Does it give you a horripilation?' and grins. 'I've been wanting to give that to you. The word, I mean. It describes the bristling of follicles. It's good, isn't it? Even if it's EmPath.'

'Yes, yes, it's good.' I laugh and remember who he is and his light touch, his stroke of genius, which makes me forgive him everything. And this time he ran a word over my skin and all the hairs stood on end. So maybe it wasn't professligacy because now I'm ready to tell him everything, the whole plan.

'Stillwell,' I say, 'that doctor robbed Eda-Lyn of her hide and dressed it in his words.' I point to the gold lettering, *Elementary Treatise on Human Anatomy*, on the book cover. 'My father pinched her, woke her up to her own story by pasting in the *Fork in the Medicine Tree*.'

He looks perplexed and then says, 'Your father took illegal possession of the book?'

'Yes.'

'And *The Fork in the Medicine Tree* is …'

'A history of the rivalry between physicians and surgeons for corpuses.'

He looks excited at that, but I can't pause now. 'With Eda-Lyn I stole away from silence. Now I need to break and enter a new language.'

'I don't understand,' he says.

'We need to thieve unbranded LipService. Not just enough for us. A whole consignment.'

'We can't just get that from Wordini … we'd have to …'

'I know – breach production.'

The idea worms a trail through the fruit of his brain. 'What do you want with so many patches?'

'Programme them.'

'With what?'

'Literat …urge …' There's a latch in my throat and it's closing. The patch is drained.

Compared to the grand kleptocrazy planned, a bit of LipService fraud is a pilfering affair, reasons Stillwell. He's suggested I patch into EmPath. Then at least it won't be so obvious if we run into anyone that I'm from 'the other side of the bed curtain'. Luckily, Bromide has recently issued a limited number of tweaked patches for peer review before the reformulation's submission for beta testing on the brand market. The test transdermal would still be programmed for EmPath, and Stillwell said he doubted the latest quip van wrinkle was much more than a 'triggered stimulant release' Bromide had been working on. That was until the doctor personally expressed his professional delight at the lab tech's participation in the testing. Now Stillwell isn't so sure about the tweak. But since he has to write the report on it, it's probably still best if he uses the trial and terror transdermal and I take the conventional one from his allocated supply.

I've locked myself in the bathroom because I don't want him to see how his transdermal gives me anxieties. 'Physician reveal thyself. Physician reveal thyself,' runs like a chant daring the bogeyman to appear in the mirror instead of my own face. Will You rise from the bled anew, transformed into a blood-letter? If I think about it any more I'll lose my vagus nerve. There is no other way; I must go undercover of the patch.

I lose my gravitational moorings in the vomit comet of disorientation but that passes faster than usual. Already, this patch feels different to the consumer brands. There's a cloy-alloy to its oily tasture that moves down my neck like a multiplying series of brass collars, telescoping my head away from my shoulders. The plinth of metal chokers my chin rests on disconnects me from the soft organic squelchings of my body. I am aware of my cross-modal interactions and gustatory hallucination but am detached from such things. From up here, I coolly survey the bathroom. I observe its intubated systems, their metabolic mechanics and borborygmi. So vice-like is their hold on my attention that I don't even notice You at my shoulder until You say, 'Now you see with a clinician's hyperopia.'

Outside the bathroom, I see Stillwell, or at least the interacting biochemical stewings that go by that name. I note an increased respiratory rate and pupil dilation. This unexpected metabolic shift doesn't escape my surgical scrutiny. 'Adverse effects?' I ask.

'With prosthetic languages, the leaking of silicone contents into the tissues is as common as with mammoplasty augmentation,' says the imbalanced organism, which then appears to suffer retroperistalsis. It recovers, thrusts something at me and says, 'Remember the aims of this operation?'

Eda-Lyn's black-ink tentacles slide over my skin and draw me down from my abstracted anatomical attitude. During the bus ride to the hospital manufactory, I keep my hand inside my canvas bag, resting on the damp squid of her hide to remind me how medicine's nitrous-oxide highs are my downfall. It's harder than I thought to resist that cerebral serene – even You are content to be drawn into its perfect analytical composure. How does Stillwell manage? I reach to taste the warm milk of human kindness in his hand.

17

We walk across the hospital manufactory grounds. Because Stillwell might be recognised, I'll have to discourse as the senior clinician. He'll be the faceless flunky with his head hidden behind a load of boxes he's carrying that are labelled as Bromide's reformulated transdermal. I don't know how he arranged for those to be ready for him at the manufactory depot or how he got my fake identity card. I had no way to ask before patching into EmPath, and now he's instructed me to 'Engage in echolalia as it'll assist in overlearning'. So I repeat my doctor's script after him, memorise his apparatchat. He's afraid that, despite being conversant in health care, I might not use the right tourniquet of phrase at the right moment.

I pall into silence as we approach the entrance to the dubway – the underground railway that transports unbranded patches from the hospital manufactory to programming sites. I've tried so many patch brands but I never really managed to stay in character. I doubt I can doctor my persona now.

Stillwell peeps around his tower of boxes. 'It's not acculturation, Frith. Just role play.' There's that bilious bobbing in his throat again as he says it. I want to ask him about his presenting problem but we're already at the transdermal scanners.

They're much the same as the one at Wordini's office for detecting patch signatures. Stillwell promised that, with our EmPath patches, getting through them would be as easy as freezing a verruca. And it is. After I've passed through, I watch him come through behind his box camoufaçade. It occurs to me for the first time that the containers will register as empty, as he's told me they are. But they don't. The guard waves him through without looking at him, and I see the computer terminal register the contents as 'EmPath/experimental'. I can't begin to understand how he did it. I had never before really grasped the power Stillwell has to talk to and command machines.

The registration counter is ahead. This causes extreme vasoconstriction of my peripheral vessels, and tachycardia. The fear makes me slip into counting beats per minute. I resist but then let the pulses of the sinoatrial node thump everything into affectlessness. It's a step forward to the counter but back from myself.

I announce myself: 'Dr Limsey. These experimental transdermals and I require neurotransmission across the synaptic gap to communicate with programming staff.'

'Research project code?' asks the foreign culture from inside the Petri dish cubicle.

Stillwell drilled me on this even while I was disenlangauged, making me repeat the eleven-digit code silently in my mind so that my head was as full of meaningless noise as my useless voice.

'No booking has been recorded for that code.'

I lean into the window and I'm surprised at my own – *our* own – authoritarian menace. 'You're not going to impede scientific progress with a case of hysterical paralysis caused by psychogenic conflict with your hypochondriacial protocols, are you?' The guard sits transfixed by your and my double glare. We are the twin serpents of the caduceus, entwined around the medic's staff. He still appears utterly immobile but there is a click as the electric doors down to the platform slide open. I stride through without a backward glance at Stillwell. But I hear his soft voice.

'Just as Dr Bromide would've done it.'

The train is already at the station being loaded by workmen. One or two move a muffling hand to mouth, making the mute sign in deference to a doctor. It kindles the remember-ember of Poppy at Lost Property and I snap out of your pathological tunnel vision.

'Stop the visual fixation,' hisses Stillwell as I continue to stare at the tongue-denied workers. 'It's a contractual requirement. If they're not refractory aphasics, they receive intravenous language blockers – as a security measure. A doctor would know that.'

We board the carriage directly behind the driver's cab, where only a small space isn't loaded with unbranded LipService and we can sit on fold-down seats. Neither of us says anything. I look out the open door at the track on the other side of the platform and notice scrawlings on the wall: 'Fuck politics', 'Wait here for further instructions' and 'Your mum smell'. Stillwell follows my glaze and says, 'Pre Lingua Quietus.' It can't be. No one who had never come of haemorrh-age would write such spitty speech gobs. Why would they? They could write anything. Besides, these were the people who wrote books.

There's bleeping and the carriage doors slam shut. The train lurches forward. Like a coin on the tracks, my belief in the redeeming power of unbranded language is flattened. These scratchings are nothing like the whirligig words in books.

The lights in our carriage flash tonic-clonic and then fail. I hear the bruxism of feet on floor. Stillwell clicks on a pocket torch and makes a superior sagittal incision in the nearest box. He pulls out unbranded transdermals and returns to orthopneic position next to me. The torch is pinched between patellae and he appears to be tussling with himself, his right hand grappling with the left shoulder. 'Probably a body identity disorder. Xenomelia? Neuroimaging of the parietal cortex could be instructive,' You say. Suddenly, he produces his torn-off patch and holds it up in the torchlight before doubling it over and stuffing it in his lab coat pocket. So it was no mental disorder – he was just wrestling to get the patch off from under his clothing. But You're quick to retort, 'Eliminating one pathology doesn't exclude the presence of another.'

Stillwell drops an unbranded transdermal into my lap before sliding off his seat onto his hands and knees on the carriage floor. You note dyspnoea. But his breathing gradually returns to normal. He rocks back on his heels and props himself against the wall, making no attempt to get back on the fold-down seat.

The torch is off and the darkness heavily bandages my eyes. There is only the dialysis-machine rush and clack of our movement along the track. With no presenting problems, no symptoms or observable behaviours to attach to, You are an embolus adrift, unable to block my natural flow. I make use of the opportunity to pull off the EmPath patch and apply the one Stillwell gave me from the box. I wait for raw language to seep into my skin.

We reach a station and the light screeches into my eyes as the brakes are applied. Stillwell squints at me. 'That patch. You should know … He did it – your cross-talk. Between sensory systems.'

'Hmmmm,' I say, still in the blurbage between patches.

'Tastures. You call it tastures. Bromide has managed to cook them into his experimental transdermal.'

The word-fuzz is gone. I stare at him.

'When I said certain things before, like "prosthetic languages", or thought them loudly enough. There was a gustatory hallucination … tastes in my mouth.'

His voice is low, stooping beneath hearing until it's struck down mute. Two dumb picker-packers come wheeling into our carriage and start loading boxes onto trolleys. We try not to look at the plundered one. As if not looking will have the same effect on them as their silence has on us. The men leave. We are still stiffened in feigned boredom when the train starts to move again.

I get up and push the incriminating box so it slips back, half toppling onto a shorter stack behind it. When I turn around again, he's not following my movements, not flame-faced for failing to hide the box immediately after opening it. Anger rises like a peppery tasture. Again the tunnel black is absolute; all my sentience is in my skin. It reminds me of the blind tastings I did. I stumble towards the wall and Stillwell.

'I'm sorry,' he says, 'I came apart under the patch's aversion therapy. Even speaking EmPath, it was as if my mouth was fixed to the end of a hospital suction hose and the gargle of necrotic flesh, pus, blood or mucus … it decomposed me. Every time I used marginal, barely permissible words like "role play" or thought unspeakable ones. Every time I focused on what we're doing. I gulped at the sickening stuff.'

'Why would Bromide make a patch with horrible tastures? Not even true ebrandgelists would buy into it. There'll be no market for it.'

'Of course, there were rewards when I stuck closely to EmPath script.'

'Just desserts.'

'Yes, custard and doughnuts. But with what we're doing, what we're planning, it was all heaving retchingness. I couldn't go on.'

'It's the perfect way to subjumate minds to a brand. Any failure to keep to the lines is punishable by potty mouth.'

'Dr Bromide will be able to retire on this transdermal technology. The corporations will be queuing up.'

I reach out for the body heat that is the life behind his voice. 'That's why we're doing this. So everyone can see there are other ways with words.'

I say this but I can't stop worrying at the scabby inscriptions on the wall of the station where we boarded. My own counterargument is that people didn't know then how narrow the passages of language could become. Not like us. That's why we'll do better. We must do better.

We sit together in the sombre sightlessness without speaking, like words lodged in a dark throat. Even with the unbranded LipService, neither of us seems to want to talk. We wait to reach Reactor Station where we'll burst forth with our new lyricism.

Stillwell has chosen Reactor Station as our destination because, like the chemicals manufacturer that is its namesake and the programming hub's biggest corporate client, most of the other businesses served are also industrials with limited LipService needs. As a result there are only two permanent programmers who execute patch edits. One for each of us to take on.

'There's no other way for us to get them to slurrender the language-programming consoles?' I ask as the lights of Reactor Station appear at the end of the tunnel.

'No. It's better if they're not just incapacitated but unconscious. And they'll recover – just like you did. Besides being minimally invasive, this procedure produces cryptogenic results – anyone using the dubway, including operators and mute picker-packers, could be responsible.'

I notice he keeps slipping into EmPath even though we're both patched into unbranded LipService.

In the goods lift up from the platform, we take off the white coats and pack them into the boxes that Stillwell is still carrying. When the doors open, we step into an automated receiving area.

Idle conveyor belts run through gates in a wall where the boxes are scanned for damage and their barcodes checked against the manifest. There's no one around.

I can't see how we can get to the programming terminals from here, but Stillwell has already stepped forward to the keypad alongside a door in a corner of the receiving area. He has pulled out his tablet and his fingers row over the black pond like long-legged water striders. He has beautiful fingers.

'I've entered your biometrics into the access system,' he says. 'Press your ear into the gel pad and the door will open. When it does, you'll have to be quick.'

I look at the greenish jelly in a square dish that is attached to the wall by an electrical wire. As my ear sinks into the slime, it oozes soapily into my orifices. I want to spit up the tasture but the door has clicked open and Stillwell is pushing me through it.

My arm pumps the air as I charge across the small office to the programmer furthest from the door. With its backing peeled off, the unbranded transdermal whirbrates *whhyyyyy* in my hand. He half turns on his chair to see me in a headlong howling to plant the patch on his neck. It sticks, but now his arms are up and we are both tangled in a scrabbling, scratching scrap as he tries to tear if off and I try to stop him. Maybe it's the adrenaline or the two-patch chemistry, but his skin is quinine bitter and I clamp my jaw against the urge to spill him out from the lock of teeth and arms. Then I feel him pull taut as a snagged thread, his legs extend straight and the air grunts out its escape from his constricted chest. As I pull him clear of the chair and onto the floor, the clonic phase of the seizure starts. His eyes have turned into his skull to search for the poltergeist in the brain that jerks and slams limbs and twitches the curtains of the face. It's better that way. This is how I must've looked in the book repository reception. I wouldn't want to watch my body do this.

'Turn him onto his side when it stops,' says Stillwell, who is sitting over the second programmer. 'Then bind his hands with this,' he continues, tossing a cable tie. 'You can also remove the patch. They'll experience extreme somnolence and not wake for at least an hour. The restraints are just to be safe.'

'Why did it work faster than when I double-patched?'

'Well, you used two commercially edited transdermals, not pure language. Plus, you had done a lot of brand switching.'

We leave the two programmers lying spent on the floor, turned on their sides facing away from the terminals. I'm tasked with scanning Eda-Lyn's pages for input while Stillwell builds to the keystroke that will let literature bleed into a batch of patches. Eda-Lyn is inky in my fingers. I think of all the tongues that I'll turn black with her printed words. And what comes over me is grand mal of glee – a beatific neural fire.

18

Two days later and we're celebrating successfully sabotaging LipService by gorging ourselves on blini, sour cream, caviar and pure language. At Reactor Station, we filled Stillwell's boxes with the literary patches and returned to the dubway, where we swapped them for the contents of unbranded patches destined for copywriters.

'I heard that a copywriter came in today accusing the manufactory of "putting a spoke in his speak" by programming unbranded patches,' says Stillwell.

My mouth is full of beluga, so all I can do is wriggle my roes and squeak in excitement that my lit service is working.

'You're not glad. You can't be. This is *not* what we wanted.' He looks at me but my *schadenfreude* takes a scarred-line attitude. 'What about showing them "the other ways with words" – what can be done with language free of branding?'

'It's just one copywriter, Stillwell. They weren't all going to say along with the literary programming.'

'What if there's an investigation?' he asks.

'There's always an investigation. Mother wants a child – there's an investigation. Mandatory post CVA-testing – an investigation. Electrodes in the brain – an investigation. I spit on your investigations.'

He scoops eggs on a finger and bubbles burst black in his mouth.

Two weeks later, Stillwell tells me about the mirror-mired. I think he is trying to get me as panicked stationary as he is. Then I see one at the mall. A woman standing in front of a mirror in a fashion retailer. She's wearing the A-Way car rentals uniform and swaying to and fro. As the patch between her eyes almost touches the glass, she spits indecipherables, then retreats into more distant mutterings.

I can't hear what she's saying but I don't need to. I can read her forewords and aft'words. The A-Way copywriter is suckling our literary LipService, so her brand speak has become imp-patched. She's trying to summon her A-Way self because she has no I without You. Stillwell says there are more and more of them. I'm too succour-punched to watch but then remember this could easily be Mother. I look up to see the woman slam her forehead into the mirror. It cracks and splits the transdermal on her head.

I am back at work but this is my armafelon, my riotous end of phrase. Sooner or later Dr Bromide will come for me and take me away, contractually bound and gagged. It's an inevitability. So why should I put my words to the flame and burn myself out for Wordini? No, I'm on a glow slow. I keep my flickerings up my sleeve as armnotes. The copywriter gave me a new project yesterday, to create sensory hook-ups for an investment portfolio. I'm not sure if it's even a real assignment or just a contradiction in tastures he has devised to get me chasing my fail. I've made a few notes about the challenges involved. I don't plan on doing more.

I'm preparing my last words and testament, what I'll bequeath to my unsaid self. Wordini's shadow scuds across my cubicle's screen wall. Stepping through the opening, he stands pinching at the vertical crease in his trousers as if trying to convince himself of its reality.

'The copies, the copies,' he says, adding urgently, 'We are going to examine them.'

What copy? I haven't written any. Then I notice that the single uptight pleat has now transferred itself to his forehead. I suppose he means the investment portfolio job but it's clear his defining line is evading him. I hesitate to answer.

'Is it not an indispensable part of a scrivener's business to verify the accuracy of her copy, word by word?' He does his best to sound threatening, but any interrogatory force whiplashes back over the language that lacks all copywriterly ka-pow. I have an oh-ho of recognition – Wordini's lit-servicing Herman Melville's story *Bartleby*. He's word-for-wording the narrator's lines. The sharp crease is now ironed into his tongue. And I put it there with my Herman Malevillent. It gives me a donkey anar-kick of 'mulish vagary'.

to the book repository fills that tiny space like a carp in a goldfish bowl. I let her print me.

For the first time in almost a year, I'm not wearing hospital pyjamas. My fingers only want to know the ricotta whey of my shirt. When I'm released from the linen cuffs, I can't stop ploughing the guava furrows of my corduroys. The door to my cell opens and I walk out. Just like that. I keep looking over my shoulder, looking for orderlies, lawyers, doctors, copywriters, she that's me. There's no one. I leave virtually unheeded.

I notice the change in LipService. Bromide's tasture technology has reached the market. Now it's easy to see, across a room, a street or office, which tout has shifted ever so slightly off-message. The bad taste it leaves in their mouth is hard to hide. They pull their faces into the ugliness of a used handkerchief. The doctor has made sure that no one can look *sprilow* while off brand. I see it in the way people try to shoot words like ping-pong balls between the teeth without letting them touch sides. At corner stores, the chewing gum stands have signs saying, 'No stock. On order.' People chew against the bitter dictates of taste. I try not to step in the pale blobs of ZapperMint, AniseIce and CinnaMax on the pavement.

I'm glad to get back to my flat. The *crepulet* palpitations of hard sell LipService on the streets and on the bus deliver me bruised and sweating onto my doorstep. Inside, I find all the Fabergé nest eggs and the piled-high attempts to regain purchase on materialism, under Wordini's instruction. I almost go straight back out again. I just want all of that gone. I need to know my walls – what to line up against, like in my cell. The boxes stack up and are tracked down the stairs to the kerb. Slowly as the flat empties, I sense my boundaries.

In the kitchen, the fridge has been switched off and cleared out but stinks. Neither here nor anywhere else in the bedsit has my life been unpacked in a great rummagery. There was no frantic search; they knew where to look: the broom cupboard door hangs defeated. Pieces of the broken robotic vacuum cleaner where I hid Eda-Lyn lie on the floor. Of course, my share of the stolen

21

In that cell, after the trial, I lost all whyfor. There was no reason in being. My pieces no longer fitted; they had grown apart. Once I woke in my cot to my screamed sentence – 'I pay for Lip Disservice; I hang my tongue in shame.' In my nightmare, I was shouting something else, but those words were the only ones possible out loud. As I lay there, something took shape in the dark umbrage I felt towards all patched expression – the word *morth*, my first shadow word. It's undefined. It bites the lip instead of serving it. It means nothing to anyone but me. I created its sound and its sense. It's entirely mine. No more second-hand language for me. Slowly, slowly, I'm adding to the shadow words – *perguiling* my vocabulary. Eventually, when I ramble, it won't be on the treacherous lie of the land.

It's weeks, maybe a month later that a copywriter with the page name Verbociter comes to speak to me. She says that, among a certain 'coterie of copyrati', my LitService has 'revived interest in leveraging book resources for brand differentiation'. As a result, a liberarian is once again needed at the repository to meet this demand.

I listen to how her ugly club-footed words make her stump speeches. Of course, she says, there's 'no rewriting the wrong': I am still condemned to my sentence. She has, however, discovered that the terms of my conviction make provision for a *parole d'honneur* spoken by a suitable corporate champion and has lobbied her association to apply. All the 'dread tape' has been taken care of. She just needs to scan my fingerprints as consent.

I think of that other contract in Dr Bromide's office and I try to read the document on her device. She lets me but my mind is as small a lurk-hole as my cell, and neither can accommodate legal furniture. Besides, just the thought of getting out and returning *convictus* will now intact her sentence.'

An orderly applies a patch to my neck and releases the restraints on my hands and feet before pulling me to my feet. A second stands by. They wait as I hunch over the jolt.

'Now, let us hear the *vox veritas*. Speak!' orders Judge Mannix.

I don't want to. I won't. The orderly thumps me on the back as if I were choking and the words fall out like half-chewed meat: 'I pay for Lip Disservice; I hang my tongue in shame.'

The crowd mocks and caterwauls. Are those even words they're hurling? The knives are out again. Used transdermals pelt down. The hissing and booing drowns out the judge, who is reading the rest of the sentence regardless. There's a brownish smudge on the adhesive side of the patch that's landed at my foot. Meaning won't stick any more.

I don't sleep at night. Stillwell knew where the book was hidden. No one else. Stillwell, the head of the forensic investigation. Stillwell my friend. I feel the hum come on all electric. The pound of blood and beating sashimi fist.

Orderly rubber soles squeak against the new polish of morning, scuffling me into the chair and dullness. Benzo days. I sit in court unminded. What I remember is madness mongering. Mrs Mondaine, my teacher of long ago, was called and arrived accompanied by a class of children dressed for a brand-mascot parade. One had a live LipService Polly Parrot. It mimicked everything being said

'Sentencing today, so no benzo,' says the orderly. 'The Surgeon Legal wants you of sound mind.' He thinks that's funny. In the Ether Jar, my wheelchair is turned for the first time to face the judge's operating table rather than the gallery.

Judge Mannix begins reading, 'As ruled *ab initio*, the defendant has been found guilty by the *processus per inquisitionem* on the counts of breaking and entering into EmPath Industries' property, the misappropriation of *materia medica* and tampering therewith, joined with the charge of compelled self-defamation pursuant to the consumption of said contaminated *materia* by members of the Copywriters' Association.'

He takes a deep breath before continuing. 'This *incursus* on our *modus vivendi* cannot be tolerated. Of courts, *culpae poenae par esto* – the punishment must fit the crime. In proclamaring her sentence every time she speaks, the felon shall *maledictio* herself and it shall memento her *ignominia* and be *horribile dictu* for all to hear. This sentence was written curtsy of the Copywriters' Association and shall be read by their *representatus*.'

Now that I face the judge, I have to twist against the restraints to see that it's Wordini who rises from his seat in the front row of the gallery and reads my sentence: 'I pay for Lip Disservice; I hang my tongue in shame.'

He lets a black tongue droop out of his mouth so that the crowd recedes from it like a hairline.

Once Wordini is seated again, the judge announces, 'The felon questioning – someone who seems to have no interest in upstaging or downcasting him. 'And *quod erat demonstrandum* the defendant's *crimen*?' Before Stillwell can answer, the procurator realises his mistake in asking something that demands more than a monosyllable. 'Allow me to refaze,' he says, his hand dramatically raised. 'Did you uncover prima facie?'

'Yes.'

'Is this your *res ipsa loquitur*?'

The 'yes' reply is softer this time, more just the sibilance of a sigh.

'*Declamatio*, please,' insists the procurator.

'Yes.'

'I present *ad curiam* Exhibit A.'

I'm in pains to see what he's talking about, but the strain is unnecessary. Procurator Brimlad moves around the room, proffering the object on a platter like wedding cake. A woman in the gallery screams and tries to clamber back over the rows above hers. Most in the crowd are confused. At first all I can see is a transparent yellowish plastic block. Then, as he moves round the arc of the gallery, I see it. Eda-Lyn is set in resin like the book in the repository's display case. Not just cast out, but cast in. Untouchable.

All my head hollows fill with weep water. Dead brackish pools no squid ink will stir. No black words from the page to murk the LipService. No way to raise a sleeve to a brine-brindled face. No, no, no. Noisy squalls that wash the sandbars of my face away. She that's more me cups her hands below my jaw to collect the run off. Her face is so terrifyingly close I can see how it's drawn on with makeup. Now, as she moulds her features with all that has leaked out of me and is lost, cheeks, chin and forehead all become more defined, more real. Already she has the scar in her eyebrow. Do I still have mine? It itches where the bare skin between the hairs should be. Soon I'll be the immaterial one. She's leaving me unsavoury, to taste of nothing.

I don't see or hear the orderly approach. Did the judge shout, call for silence? Only the bore of the needle pries into flesh and consciousness. It opens a tunnel into mind and matter that collapses on itself.

'The defendant is sedated, your Honour.'

'*Objectio* overwrought,' says the judge and waves her back to her seat.

Wordini's triumphant finger-kissing opens up a fault in me, and I half stand, my wrists still bound to the wheelchair's arms and start running at him. Beneath the carapace of the chair, I hear the wind between my handlebar horns. The movement is its own impetus. Until I harrow into Wordini's back. And the possessed whistling dies out.

When the orderlies come for me again the next day, they also restrain my ankles to the footrests' struts. 'Any further attempts at perverting the course of justice and it's sedation for you,' says the hairy one who had been escorting Wordini out when I charged at him.

Wordini's advertorial outburst still seems to be ringing in people's ears, leaving them deaf to new sounds. Petula sits listlessly swiping a device screen while she rubs a foot with the other hand. Again and again, Judge Mannix a-hems, everyone sits up blinking, but he fails to call the court to order. When the session finally begins, Procurator Brimlad summons Stillwell to the stand.

It's wrenching trying to see his face, but he stays turned away as he walks to the witness chair. The collar of his white coat is turned up against the cold, or everything else. I feel how he is buttoned up and I'm afraid – I don't know whether for him or me. Pivoting in my chair, I glimpse the orderly, who rocks on the balls of his feet and raises a finger. I sit quietly to hear what Stillwell will say. Can't let them banish me into the n-ether now.

'You were the *facile princeps* of the *posse forensis* that investigated the medico-tempering of LipService patches?'

'Yes.'

'The *onus probandi* – the burden of proof – was on this posse. And what evidence did you discover? Did *veritate triumpho*?'

'Yes.'

'Your posse revelared that the *programma* was sorcered from the *index librorum prohibitorum*.'

'Yes.'

At last, the procurator has a witness ameekable to his

'Could we continue?' asks Procurator Brimlad. 'Is it not a non sequitur to employ a persona non grata in essential surfaces such as copywriting?'

'Perhaps to the sparrow-minded,' says Wordini, looking directly at the procurator. 'But the best way to mortar a maverbrick into place is to turn oddity into commodity. Which is why my medicronies and I are launching Censory LipService – a patch that brings your speech to your senses ...'

Wordini's announcement whooshes through the gallery that had been wilting under all the hot air.

'Copywriter, copywriter ...' insists the procurator, hoping to switch Wordini's raillery back onto his track, but he rattles on, overfreighted.

'Imagine dining out on your brand slogan. You can – but can you guess how it will taste? This is the real lip-smacking nature of the desplendent's perversity and now you can safely relish the deviant neural paths that brought her here.'

The audience bends to his windy language.

'Our Censory LipService lets you savour word flavours.'

'*Contemptus!*' bellows the judge. 'The court is not a forum for *mercators* to *vender* their *vendibles*. You will adhere to the question or be held in *contemptus*.'

Wordini is undeterred. 'Free sample patches sponsored by The Hayrick at the exit.' The judge responds with the knee-jerk action of the reflex hammer. An orderly reaches under each of the copywriter's armpits, and together they haul him away, still inveigling, 'With Censory LipService, you'll truly chew over your words, as never before!'

The crowd are shifty in their seats, furtively turning to the exit, where another pair of large orderlies has stepped forward to block the doors. As Wordini is dragged past me, he succeeds in bringing the digits of one hand to his mouth and kissing them in a gesture that is part ironic *magnifique* – perhaps, at all that has brought me to this point – and part finger-licking. It's what I also saw Dr Bromide do.

'Your Honour, Surgeon Legal, I haven't cross-interrogoed the witness,' complains Petula Ormod.

20

In my cell, I lie on my bed, digesting the yoghurty tasture of the sheets. It's proof of life when I'm starting to feel unreal. Language in the Ether Jar sublimates into gas, increasing the empty spaces between atoms of meaning. I am that void, the unspoken, the rapidly dispersing significance of these speech particles.

Words fail me. They do me no justice. Not because I am innocent, but because they can't give offense – least of all mine. What does the procurator or Judge Mannix or Petula Ormod or Dr Bromide think my patch prose was like? What does the unspeakable mean to those who have never heard it – like the mob eager to lynchpin it on me? Do they even know what *it* is? In LipService there is rhyme but no reason.

There is someone who could tell everyone what LitService was really like, who knows what it's like to face a dead wall of language. And when I return to the Ether Jar on Monday, he is called to testify. I can tell from the crease in his trousers that he has returned to the fold.

'Copywriter,' says the procurator, 'you are the provisor of *panem et circenses* to the *plebeius* …'

'Bread and circuses!' interrupts Wordini. 'Who writes your Arguendo? That is just too ah-cute.'

'Arguendo is an *imperium in imperio*,' mumbles Brimlad. 'Now, forthwith to the *quaestio*: What confeasible interest could you have in this offender?' He waves towards me.

'Commercial, of course. The good doctor and I reached our mutually agreeable firms on merchandising. *Manus manum lavat* and all that. Isn't that what you lawyawners say – one hand washes the other?'

The audience starts applauding, Wordini takes a bow, and the procurator rams the witness chair into the back of his knees so that he falls back into his seat.

Mum fatale has told them about how I tried to get her to use unprogrammed LipService.

'Oh, yes. There's no merrywidow with her, it's all boxer nastiness. My daughter is ill fitting and rides up my back because of it. It was chest-bindingly cruel to force that unbranded pastie onto me. I would never go commando, I always wear my Frisson Froufrou. But do you think I sagged a bit? No.'

The procurator is standing just in front of me, bordelloed over. I don't think he understood a word but he's rushing over to her. My neck snaps round to follow him and for the first time I look at Mother sitting in the witness chair with the procurator on his knees to her right, clasping her hand. On her left the judge crouches, clutching her other hand. The light from the dome above illuminates the rose raincoat and Mother is transfigured into the madonna of the sunset corona. She's a woman on fire, and through the glow I swear I see she-me standing behind Mother, arms over head, holding the lighter aloft. Mother is the brand made flesh, Frisson Froufrou incarnate. The men of law are weak-kneed before her.

Petula stamps her foot but it makes no sound in its hushed-up hose. '*Objectio, objectio!*' The judge hurls the reflex hammer at her but it glances off her bunched shoulder pad. I start laughing. It's an ugly sound, but I can't stop.

When order is finally restored and the adorers have regained their feet, the procurator says, 'The *testimonium* of this charming gentlewoman is *lux in tenebris*, a great illuminator. For what does it reveal?' He pauses uncertainly.

I see them all waiting on the gallery's hard wooden benches, waiting to understand and participate in the court's catharsis. For once they aren't all looking at me, and I search the rows for Stillwell, but he's not there.

'What does it not reveal!' he declares triumphantly.

With that court is adjourned for the weekend.

quia absurdum est. The defendant's *innocentia* is shelf-evident because it is absurd. Can you deny this, Doctor?'

Bromide makes a strange spitting noise and Petula pirouettes back to her seat.

Most mornings the wheelchair comes for me and I sit in the courtroom. I try to listen but the words circle like water-bloated food in a blocked sink. Sooner or later I etherise into the upper reaches of the dome. The light changes. There is the occasional passage of birds, a plane. Clouds *accumulo* and nimbus. Down below, the words swill round and round.

After breaking for lunch, the procurator calls a new witness.

There's a sound like a body bag being moved. Mother appears wearing a red-trimmed, transparent pink raincoat over a knee-length black shift dress. Red manicured nails hold the edge of the hood over her head as if a sudden sousing gust might blow it back. Mother knows how to make an entrance. The bare skin of her arms simpers through the rose-coloured PVC. She sits in the witness chair behind my right shoulder. I refuse to turn and look at her.

The bailiff orderly swears her in: 'Do you swear on the power of speech invested in the transdermal and pains of a second cerebral haemorrhage to tell the truth, the whole truth and nothing but the truth?'

'I do.'

'Madame,' says the procurator, who hasn't been nearly so gracious in addressing previous witnesses, 'you are the defendant's *mater familias*, correct?'

'Yes,' she whispers in her most tragic voice.

'Perhaps you could provide a dictum about the *lapsus linguae* inflicted on you?'

'Oh sir, I'm afraid you're going for the absolute opaques and leaving it all to the imagination.' I don't need to look to know she's producing a full ingénue's blushfulness.

'The unbranded LipService in *flagrante delicto*,' explains the procurator.

'Schizophasic cretins,' says Bromide softly. He is seated just behind my right shoulder and my restraints Chinese-bangle my skin as I turn to see if anyone else heard. He holds my gaze and raises his fingers, which are curled together like the legs of a dead spider as he carefully licks each one. I don't know what this message means, but seeing him use a form of mute point condenses like the horror and stench of a stranger's breath at your neck in the night.

The procurator is trying to pick up on his wavering line of questioning. 'And what would you say, doctor, is *per definitionem* the *composition mentis* of the defendant?'

I don't care to hear about my state of mind, and neither does she that's not me, who is sitting spinning in circles on the polished parquet floor. I slump and let the backrest of the wheelchair strike a blue to my head as I rush for the dome of sky. If I could sink my arms elbow-deep into that ether, how would it taste? Of absinthe and ease, louche clouds. This is what I'll take back to the cell. I've managed not to think of it before. But now it clangs dinner slot, breakfast slot. Time slot. Under the thumb of the dust beneath the bed. Still humming electric even though the wiring is definitely loose.

'*Silentium! Silentium!* The defendant is *vox nihili*. Any further *disruptionem* and sedation will be required. This is the Ether Jar.'

Luckily the humming stops. Looking around for the source, I find the proxymate in the audience again. She-me flicks a lighter, singeing the hair of the woman seated in front of her. The filament snake-dances in the flame before coiling up into a fiddlehead fern. How can I possibly see this from metres away? I am not her. I am not the one who sets heads ablaze, even if I had hoped to.

Petula Ormod is called to cross-examine Dr Bromide the next day. She stands and I notice that she has no shoes on, only stockinged feet. Blazing bunions, undimmed even by the haze of hose, apparently explain this. I'm afraid Petula Ormod is a woman always before a hump. The condition of her jacket remains unchanged. '*Nolo contendere* – there is nothing to contest,' she begins. 'Nevertheless, I argue that the doctor must conceit, *credo*

'Guilty, however you slice it, so give us our cut ...' says a voice from the upper gallery. A giant foam hand with a pointing index finger printed with SUE-VENIRS waves briefly, but before the speaker can finish, the hammer has fallen and the boot reflexively struck.

Judge Mannix continues: 'Procurator Brimlad will now furbish the evidence of *culpa verbatim*, whereupon the defence counsel will *respondeat*. Thereafter, all that remains is for the court to deliver *sententiae severitatis*.'

I fold, dog-eared at the sudden firecracker outbursts. Quiverbangs of words, too loud, too many, come from all directions. I am uncountenanced. My features stare accusingly at me from the third row. She that's not me. Un-me. Me. If I'm edited out of existence, will she go on without me and live the life of a brandit as if I never was? It's either drop my gaze into my lap or lift it to the dome above. I choose to dome out.

In between the metal spokes that hold the glass, I can arrange the wheeling words. And when I've spun it all out, I am guilty. Oh well. I knew that. So here I am sitting at *The Fork in the Medicine Tree*, where barbery-surgery assumed bookish tones and reasoned what to do with our bodies.

That voice, the one speaking now, it smears iodine orange. I turn to see Dr Bromide.

'It was established that the biometric reading of the right pinna gel impression recorded at the entrance to the Reactor Station programming hub produced a false positive on identity. Based on helix, lobule, tragus, fossa and other geometries, a search through our biometric databases was conducted and a match found,' he says.

'Let us bear *in memoriam*, this heinous act of *crimen fals*i, knowingly committed ...' says the procurator, before being interrupted by the witness.

'Are you not interested in the patient match?'

'*Quaestio* is the sole preservative of the court,' reprimands the judge.

'Veritably, veritably,' says the flushed procurator.

row, on either side of the centre aisle running up the tiers. Petula looks more crushed than ever. One shoulder is higher than the other, as if the pad on that side of the jacket had curled into a defensive ball. A tissue waives the white flag from the sleeve that hangs longer.

One of the orderlies escorting me steps forward into the amphitheatre and announces, 'All incise for the honourable Judge Proctor Mannix.' The audience dutifully stands and hacks at the deeply notched benches in front of them with little plastic scalpels that were handed to them as they filed in. 'For every rewrite, there is a remedy; where there is no remedy, there is no rewrite,' intones the orderly bailiff. Behind me, the judge is taking his place at the wooden operating table when a man in the audience wearing a huge purple top hat with a sign above saying SUE-VENIRS leaps up and shouts, 'Give us our cut and get to keep your souvenir scalpel!'

'*Contemptus, contemptus!*' says the judge striking the operating table with a reflex hammer. '*Commercial actio* is *prohibeo* in the Ether Jar.' An orderly I hadn't noticed before on the other side of the amphitheatre responds by roughly kicking the tout out. Without turning his head, the judge then extends his arm back to beckon to the orderly still at my side, who wheels me in. There's a hiss, and dozens of arms reach out to point a plastic scalpel at me. The reflex hammer rises again and the extended limbs return to their original positions. I am parked in front of the operating table, facing the cut-thirsty. The judge begins reading aloud.

'For the benefit of the vulgaris, and their instruction in *bonos mores*, the court will present its findings as per the *processus per inquisitionem* into the counts of breaking and entering into EmPath Industries' property, the misappropriation of *materia medica* and tampering therewith, joined with the charge of compelled self-defamation pursuant to the consumption of said contaminated *materia* by members of the Copywriters' Association. It is important that we start *ab initio* with the verdict: The *cogito* of the court has found the *sum* of the *ergos* point indeplorably to the guilt of the accused in *mens reas* and *actus reus*.'

'This will be our only consolation,' she says rising and extending her hand.

It takes me a moment to realise she must mean 'consultation'. Or maybe she doesn't.

I pinch bruises on my arms to feel the days but still they leave no marks. My body won't retain even the simplest authorgraph. So there's a new series of thumbprints in the dust under my bed. More than thirty. Petula Ormod said next month, but still no one comes for me. You used to be stuck in my head but who's trapped now? Has un-me gone a-courting without me? Who'll be the judge of this? I demand an interrogation!

The door slot clangs for the clearing of the dinner plate. But in the plate's place is a pile of fabric. A message from the mutes. No, they're new, starchy pyjamas that stick stodgily to the palate. 'Tomorrow, 8am,' says a voice beyond the door.

With the clang of breakfast, I leap from sleep to frantic washing, scattering water droplets and spilling thoughts. On my third mouthful of cold porridge, the door opens. Two orderlies push in a wheelchair: 'Sit.' I wave refusing hands and hop on eloquently articulating legs, but they continue their advance. They don't stop till ranting arms and legs are bound and still. Only when I'm strapped to the chair do they set the hospital corridors rolling by me. Buckled leather clams up tight the tasture of cockles.

As I am brought to a side passage leading into the Ether Jar, the procurator, Petula Ormod and the judge are scrubbing up. 'Ah, the clean hands doctrine,' murmurs one of the orderlies reverently as I am parked in the wings with a view of the tiered semicircular gallery of public seats. Directly ahead of me is a display case containing the glass bulb and wooden mouthpiece first used in this very amphitheatre. An audience of surgeons and students witnessed the administration of ether by inhalation to render a patient insensate before surgery. The plaque says so. Overhead, a glass cupola presses outwards against that other ether, the great blue opiate for the incarcerated.

The procurator and defence counsel take their seats in the first

No, don't let me go. She'll probably give them everything, leave nothing for me. So I squeeze her gassy windpiping with its pseudo-copywriter talk. I need to speak; I need to have something left to tell. I haven't been interrogated since the day after I arrived here. I need to hear my say.

I wake to orderlies. They haul me stickily to my feet. And then I'm outside the cell, in the corridor, with a clear line of sight for twenty metres. The pull on my eyes of such expansiveness is like the tug over the railing from the fiftieth floor. I stumble. A sharp left turn into another room – this one with a window – and I stand neck-deep in the eiderdown of sunshine. The rays of hysterical happiness don't part until I hear a voice say, 'Please sit.'

There's a woman at a table, indicating the chair opposite her. 'My name is Petula Ormod. I am your defence council.' She looks at me. 'Unfortunately, your history of language offences, which speaks to your *animus noncendi* to LipService, has made it impassable for me to provide you with a transdermal. I don't require your dictum anyway. The procurator will provide me with the *ratio decidendi*.'

Her shoulder pads look as if she had received an emergency massage while still wearing her jacket. She speaks with a similar wrung-out weariness. I haven't heard words for so long, I just want to put all of them in my mouth like a one-year-old – even if they're the legal profession's Arguendo LipService. But she's ruining it for me, the way she heaves and dumps language like bags of cement.

'It has been duly derided to bring your case before your peers. A date has been set for next month. Appropriate *vestimentum* will be delivered *de futuro* for your appearance. After all, the case will be heard in the Ether Jar – the surgical amphitheatre. May I remind you, *salus populi est suprema lex*.'

I look at her blankly and shrug.

She huffs in exasperation. 'The rights of the brand take presidents over the rights of the *individuum*. The role of the law is to protect corporate identities from *crimen injuria*.'

I should ferment my anger, rise frothing, but the patch of sun holds me in yellow inertia.

19

There's that humming again. I bang the wall till my sashimi fist is just a pound of blood and the hum turns to a whimper. Then I know it was me all along, but I don't recognise myself. I'm a speaker picking up the drone of my own alternating current. She that's not me has returned to oppose me and set in motion my mind's voltaic reversals. I hum electric. I live by the rule of hum. You think that's what I would say? I am a liar and an imposter. Out, out all copyblighter's cant!

I try to keep track of the dumbstruck days with thumbprints in the dust under my bed. But she that's not me (or is she?) walks free, swaying to a warble croon. The gusting flurries of her skirts hustle up the dust and I lose time. I don't want to be alone and un-me any more.

The door slot clangs dinner. Once I crouched at the door, waiting for the slap of rubber soles and then the hand to reach in the slot and remove the empty tin plate. I just wanted the taste of something beyond the plaque scum that coats everything in this room – the cement floor, bed linen, steel basin and toilet, as well as the identical sets of pyjamas. I even deluded myself for a moment it might be Stillwell, but my palm closed around an okra wrist as mucilaginous as the fingers of the orderlies that brought me here. Before I could wince away, a fork shivved into my hand. It wasn't mine; I don't get a fork to eat with.

There she goes with my body. Three paces to the sink. The proxymate sits on the steel basin and I on the bed. Do my thighs graze ham or yoghurt? Or yogham? Aggghh – a veritverbal abomination. Forswear all hateful words in advertguise that try to be in two places at once. Stop infiltrating my hideous languish! Why do You torment me? She that's not me slips through the door – four paces to the threshold – crossing the language barrier.

The words run through me like a crack in the wall of my reveries. Is that what this is all about? Proving to me that he's beaten the programming of my patch and that he can do what I always failed to – twisting Bartleby's diction to his own bitter ends? Or is he actually using unbranded LipService and just got the necessary lines down patter in advance? It's impossible to know. And that is what will torment me.

One at each strong arm, the orderlies start shuffling me off. I see Wordini beaming, his mouth a grin as perfectly ironed across his face as the crease in his trousers.

directions. But my head is on a pillow of warm breath, and fingers of milk run through my hair.

Sitting at my desk, I'm dowsing for the sensation of resting on Stillwell's chest. Instead I hear a thick rubber sole drag squeal-heeling over the polished floor. The sound is almost as screaming as the chilli tasture of the material. I look up to see Wordini accompanied by two large orderlies at the entrance to my cubicle. One of the orderlies steps forward and leans on the back of my chair so that the hairs on his knuckles create a pucker down my spine of mouth-dryingly bitter grape seed.

'You have the right to remain silent,' says the orderly in bored tones, already tearing at the patch on my arm. 'You are under suspicion of medical tampering. You will be confined to an isolation ward until you can be taken to theatre and opened up for examination.'

The same orderly is already wrenching me out of the chair with his slippery okra palm when Wordini speaks. 'I tremble to think that my contact with the prisoner has already and seriously affected me in a mental way. And what further and deeper aberration might it not yet produce?'

He appears to be addressing the orderly, grateful for the removal of the authorn in his side. But why is he still reciting Bartleby? The orderlies must've explained things to him already. He could've dispatched my literary programming.

He continues: 'Conceive a woman by nature and misfortune prone to a pallid hopelessness.' Wordini nods at me. 'Can any business seem more fitted to heighten it than that of continually handling these dead letters …?'

He's talking to me, using my beautiful tales to try to travestate all I believe in.

'On errands of life, these letters speed to death.'

Both orderlies are starting to stamp and snort like impatient carthorses now, but the copywriter is not done yet.

He looks directly at me and says, 'Your prefer-nots have all come for you now. I'm afraid there'll be no more preferences, only assumptions.'

someone in the medical professions. But who exactly will be harder to prove. I'll be a suspect, of course. They'll want you to give me up, save them the trouble.' His voice and the quiet deliberateness of the telling have the same relationship to its implications as a doodle does to the telephone conversation that accompanies it. He doesn't ask me not to be a backblabber. And although the masque raiding and the deceptions and above all the meticulous caution behind our thievery were all his, he doesn't seem surprised at our imminent apprehension. Instead he looks at me patiently pedagogical, waiting for me to follow his trail of medcrumbs.

I decide I can't give him my unprogrammed word never to let the rat out of the bag. Bromide has pulled things, like tastures, from my head that I couldn't have told. It's only in futilfiling any hope of not squealing that I realise what will certainly be lost – our intimatey confidences, our accomplicities. Our speakeasies. His words are like my tastures – improbably and illogically announcing sensations that branded language denies. The sounds he makes are sops of the sweet, tender fleshiness of fellow feeling. I had that with Dad but his messages always had to cut corners off the pages of books.

'Is this the last time we'll be able to do this?' I ask.

'Maybe.'

'You knew this would be our bitter unfriending. So why did you agree to break into language?'

'You were determined. You would've tried, even without my help. And the result would've been the same. This way, we have a little longer and I get to show you what I believe words should do. You hold onto them as beautiful things that anyone should be able to own. I wanted you to see for yourself what happens when you give them away. We've parleyed an attachment, an ... an affection for each other. And not just based on the alignment of interests that comes from a common brand loyalty.'

Sadness makes my bones feel brittle. I don't think they can hold up against the gravity of planetary forces. 'Come,' says Stillwell and lifts my head onto his chest so that we lie in a T-shape on the uncultured carpet cheese. Our feet point in two very different

I'm listening now, toeing the storyline, impatiently anticipacing the plot's beats. He continues more confident. 'I didn't understand why. Our studies show ...'

I can hear him consciously taking the scenic route around the easy EmPath.

'I mean, we find that people who don't identify with their transdermal's brand tend to say less, not more. So when I saw one sitting in a hallway, waiting to consult with a specialist, I sat down with him. I was in a white coat and had my tablet with me. Maybe he thought I was assigned to his case; maybe he didn't care. He was happy to talk. I think I know what's happening now.'

Stillwell pauses for a dramatic reflect and I want to laugh – not at him but at the lab tech who has learned to tell stories and not just crunch data.

'When you apply a trademarked patch for the first time, you and everyone you communicate with is already familiar with the brand personality and narrative. It's why we can ... uh ... parse LipService drift. Because we know the product and selling points.'

'But no one knows the stories from my book.'

'Yes. Exactly. So the copywriters want an interlocutor to push them to unexpected answers, hoping to piece together the brand narrative from the LipService drift. They can't imagine that the language isn't based on a brand identity. Why else would someone try to hiyack their words? To have their product encoded into the transdermals of every other brand LipService is written for. It creates an absolute monopoly.'

I can tell he's very chuffpuffed with himself – and not just for having worked it all out. Probably been waiting to drop that aplomb all this time. Hiyack. It's not a bad flick of the gist, though.

'Do you think they'll realise there's no brand behind the stories?' I ask.

'Doubt it. But the programmers who are working on reverse engineering and tracing the coding might. An investigation has been launched. Sooner or later, they'll find you.'

'I suppose it was inescapable. What will happen to you?'

'That depends on you. It will be obvious that you had help from

I tell Stillwell about Wordini parroting the copyist's refrain. Exultant, I lark through my report, adding swooping-highs and diving-lows. So there's a bit of embellpolish but that's because Stillwell isn't rousing to my tale.

'You don't think Wordini deswerves to miss the point, the way the rest of us with patchwork language do – when he's the one pushing us off terse?'

'It's not that. It's ...you're as trapped in this copyist story as he is. Why can't *we* be the story?' he asks.

'What, you mean you and me?'

'I mean whichever people talk to each other.'

'And you think their narrowtives matter more?'

'To them they do. More than a brand narrative or a law scrivener story.'

'My mother proves you're wrong,' I snap.

His voice is soft as a smotherer's cushion. 'But you know that isn't what she always wanted. She adapted to sur–'

'Yes, she originally wanted to use me as a LipServant. So her story mattered more than mine.'

'But it doesn't have to be like that,' he says.

There's a long silence, a great divide between words. Stillwell speaks again first, trying to keep his tone as delicate as gauze, but my wounds went sceptic long ago.

'I know you have over-cathected the book and ...'

He's slipped into EmPath and he knows it. I can't tell what he sees but my facial muscles feel like a series of tripwires pulled taut. Any release in tension will be explosive.

'Frith, please, I'm sorry. I shouldn't have said it like that. Let me explain. You see, Wordini's not the only one.'

I know what he's trying to do, wrapping me in his pashmina pleas. But I'm not shawling for it. I just look away and say nothing.

'More and more copywriters are being brought in to the hospital. Usually by corporate clients or associates. All of them with your book patches. They come quite willingly. They want, they're desperate for conversations where someone else is in control, someone else steers the talk.'

Since I still haven't replied, Wordini says, 'You are decided, then, not to comply with my request – a request made according to common usage and common sense?'

It's no longer important whether or not he's trying to ask about the investment portfolio job. For once I know the script to his patch, while he can make as little head of its tale as the narrator. I delight in answering as the copyist Bartleby: 'I would prefer not to.'

'*Why* do you refuse?'

'I would prefer not to.'

I imagine the patch's narratively conditioned responses projected as luminous surtitles flashing up across the proscenium of his forehead. Right now it probably reads, 'I begin to stagger in my own plainest faith. I begin, as it were, vaguely to surmise that, wonderful as it may be, all the justice and all the reason is on the other side.'

He is bewildered at how my words can trap him in this theatre. He hasn't worked it out yet. So he musters new lexicality but is disarrayed again by what comes out of his mouth.

'Say now that in a day or two you will begin to be a little reasonable.'

'At present I would prefer not to be a little reasonable,' I reply in as cadaverous a tone as I can.

He is beginning to understand that he is staring at a dead brick wall of language, and, despite that, it holds him in a reverie. So much so that he walks off muttering 'prefer not to'. Prefer not to, prefer not to, prefer not to, prefer not to. He repeats this so often that the meaning of the words collapses under the weight of their sound. Pri-fur-not-to.

Long after Wordini has gone, I wonder if he receives the ministrations of a literary You. And what literary You is like. I thrill to think that You are finally a manifestation of me. That would be a mole reversal. Me as the burrowing vox provocatrix in copywriters' heads. After all those times I was heckled by corpyrited ventriloquism, that would go some way to settling the sore. Ah, shivers of a dish best served scold.

unbranded patches is also gone from the bedroom curtain hem. Not that I expect to ever speak the shadow words out loud.

Sitting on the counter drinking water from a glass – a real, menthol-chill glass, not a paper cup – I notice the Nice Slice pizza clock has stopped. I take it off the wall and pry the back open. In the compartment where the batteries should go are three unbranded patches. On each one a word is written in black marker: sorry, sorry, sorry.

At the repository, below the dirt again at last, I stand in the familiar ring of unspoken words, looking at the balconied shelves circling the silo walls. The air smells quiet. I sit. From down here, I try to imagine wrapping my mind around the many-storied bigness of it. I would be pulled far and wide, stretched tauter than Eda-Lyn to contain all those tales. I get up and go looking for her remains. Copies of all the books that got under her skin are laid out in state on the floor. I arrange and rearrange them but I can't find her flavour profile beneath my fingers. She is flat and dead, a skeleton.

The buzzer sounds in the silo. I exit the airlock to attend to the burrower. It's Verbociter. As soon as I appear she says, 'I want the one where "Echo still repeats the last words spoken."'

So I turn around and go back into the silo. All I have to do is pick up the Ovid from within that outline of a body drawn in copy on the floor. But I can't. Even though no one is allowed to remove books from the reading room, I know what Verbociter is taking away from me.

As part of our echo studies, Dad showed me a paper on how people are able to judge the distance of a sound's source. It's all about amplitude modulation and the way reverberations dampen the loud and softs. The more objects the sound waves crash against on their travels, the more echoes eddy around. In an anechoic chamber it's impossible to tell how remote a noise is. That's exactly what will happen to the story of Echo. Her voice won't carry true when it strikes up against a whole brand portfolio of products. No one will hear the dusty slap of Ovid's Roman sandals coming from far away.

The *chorteen* is already suited up, masked and waiting when I return. She snatches the book from my hand and rustles her biohazard plastic off to the reading room. When I go back into the silo, there's a movement behind a distant shelf and I feel the presence of she that's not me like an old wound in wet weather.

I wear headphones whenever I leave the flat. It looks as if I'm listening to jingles, but I just don't want to hear Verbociter's LipServiced version of Ovid's story. I try to keep words between my ears and the edges of a page. I don't speak; I don't listen. If I could I would shut my eyes, too, so no capitals on hoardings, signs and windows can pierce my thick skull with their interrobangs. And I wouldn't have to see everyone's lips curled *borchardly* back against the offensive language of my tastures.

More copywriters come to the repository, far more than I ever remember when Dad was here. They wink and tell me they want 'the one with the fellow who prefers not to' or 'to con-verse with the creature who has no toes'. Some even insist on rifling the stacks themselves. I keep watch because I can't turn my back.

On the days when I can't stand it, I imagine having a child – someone to break my silence and *skeepen* the shadow words. But I soon *meaker* again, remembering Mother, and why she had me, and all the *hepnot* past that followed. I will not repeat that. Neither will I think of Stillwell and how he would tell me a language that isn't shared isn't a language at all. But what have I ever gained from sharing? So instead I *finock* mentally through my glossary and *glinker* at each *erpish teetle*.

Acknowledgements

Thank you to the Jacana Literary Foundation for being brave enough to publish a novel about breaking through entrenched forms of expression and to my editor Jenefer Shute, whose delicate touch belies a laser-like acuity in separating the good from the bad.

While writing this novel as part of the MA in Creative Writing at the University of the Witwatersrand, I was very fortunate to have the support of Karen Lazar and Bronwyn Law-Viljoen, as well as the infinitely perceptive Gerrit Olivier. They patiently turned my words over every which way and offered sound and sane comment. The input of my fellow travellers Jessica Liebenberg, Dennis Dvornak and Billy Rivers was also invaluable. Thanks also go to my parents for their supernatural faith in me. Finally, I owe a debt of gratitude to my intrepid readers Danièlle Crouse, Vicky Jacob-Ebbinghaus and above all, my husband James.